D1272018

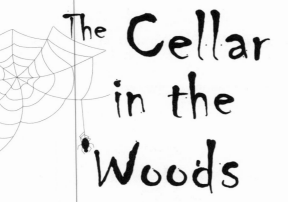

The Cellar in the Woods

By
Jacqueline Stem

EAKIN PRESS ★ Austin, Texas

FIRST EDITION

Copyright © 1997
By Jacqueline Stem

Published in the United States of America
By Eakin Press
An Imprint of Sunbelt Media, Inc.
P. O. Drawer 90159 ★ Austin, TX 78709-0159

2   3   4   5   6   7   8   9

ISBN 1-57168-115-9

Library of Congress Cataloging-in-Publication Data

Stem, Jacqueline.
    Cellar in the woods / by Jacqueline Stem.
        p.   cm.
    Includes bibliographical references.
    Summary: When twelve-year-old Joanna, her younger sister, and their cousin mark discover a haunted house in the woods, they set out to resolve the mysteries surrounding it.
    ISBN 1-57168-115-9
    [1. Haunted houses — Fiction. 2. Mystery and detective stories.] I. Title.
PZ7.S8282Ce   1997.
642' .4'09764
[Fic] -- dc21   97-40016
                                                            CIP
                                                            AC

To
Adam, Abby, Audrey, Ali,
and
Benjamin

Contents

A Discovery

I t was the first day of our vacation when we found the ruined house in the woods. It crouched under a thick blanket of vines, as though hiding from the thunder that grumbled in the distance.

The place looked creepy in the gloomy light. Its crumbling stone walls dipped to the ground on one side where the roof had caved in. The small clearing was full of weeds and wildflowers. Little pine trees and laurel bushes crowded in, slowly reclaiming the land.

I shivered.

"I have a feeling it's haunted," Sally Rachel said in a hushed voice.

Mark snorted. Sally Rachel was always "having a feeling." We didn't usually pay any attention, even though her feelings were of-

1

ten right. This time I was inclined to agree with her.

We just stood there, caught in a strange spell. Thunder crashed closer and lightning lit up the little clearing. Raindrops as big as nickels fell, slowly at first, then quickly in a downpour.

"Come on," Mark yelled. "There's enough of that place left to keep us dry."

He streaked across the clearing and disappeared into the black hole of an open doorway. Sally Rachel and I were close behind. Even the creepy ruin was better than the drenching rain.

Half of the front room was buried under the fallen roof. Beams hung over the other half like skeleton bones, offering no protection from the rain. We stumbled over the rubble into one of two back rooms, where enough of the roof was left to shelter us.

The room looked like it had been a kitchen. A filthy, cracked sink hung on one wall. A moldy table sat under the empty window. In one corner a chair slumped on a broken leg, and in another a rusted cook stove was slowly turning into red dust.

There were cobwebs everywhere. Vines pushed through the window, twisting around everything they touched. The room smelled musty and decayed. There was a mournful feeling that gave me goosebumps. I was glad to be dry, though, and we huddled together as the thunderstorm roared over us.

Sally Rachel, Mark, and I were in the piney woods of East Texas minding our Aunt Florrie's antique shop while she had some necessary surgery. Mom and Aunt Laura (Mark's mother), both teachers on summer vacation, had volunteered themselves and us to help. Except for the small vacation resort across the lake from Aunt Florrie's house, there was not much to do in this pretty but poky little place. I hoped it wouldn't be too boring.

Sally Rachel rustled around the room, too curious to stay still. She looked into and under everything she could reach.

"Better be careful, Sal. There's probably bugs under there," Mark teased.

"I'm not afraid of bugs," she snapped, tilting her sassy nose in the air.

That was true. Eight-year-old Sally Rachel Roberts probably knew more about bugs than the bug experts. She would pick up anything that interested her. Blessed with soft blonde hair, brown eyes and dainty features, she looked delicate and feminine, but that was nature's big joke. She was tomboy to the bone, with a huge curiosity and not enough fears. I

3

was forever either rescuing or making excuses for my little sister.

"Please be careful, Sally," I pleaded. "It's too far to carry you home if you get hurt."

"Don't nag, Joanna," she said sharply and kept rummaging in the corner behind the broken chair.

"Look at this, guys," she exclaimed. "There's a big ring in the floor. I wonder what it's for?"

Mark and I went to look. "Looks like a trap door to a cellar," he offered, nudging the heavy, iron ring with his toe.

"Can we lift it? I have a feeling there's something interesting down there," Sally said.

"You have a feeling about *everything,* Sally," I reminded her. "It's probably full of spiders and snakes."

Mark tugged on the ring, but couldn't lift the heavy stone.

"If you two will help me, maybe we can open it," he suggested.

We all took hold of the ring and pulled. The stone slab was very heavy, and it barely budged. After a couple of tries and a great heave, we pulled it all the way back. Underneath were narrow, stone steps going down into smelly darkness.

"Oh, look," cooed Sally Rachel. "Let's go see!"

4

"Phew! Let's don't. It stinks down there," I said nervously. "We can't see anything in the dark anyway."

Sometimes I "had a feeling" too. Mine were vague things that often didn't make any sense. The nasty smell, the dark hole at our feet, and the creepy house made me extremely uneasy.

"Here's my penlight," Mark said, producing a tiny flashlight from his pocket. "There you go, Sally. Tell us what's down there."

Until yesterday, Mark hadn't seen Sally Rachel since our joint birthday party, his thirteenth and my twelfth, almost a year ago. He probably didn't dream she would do it.

"Some cousin you are," I growled furiously. "Why don't you go see?"

"Oh, I'll be right behind you, Sally," he teased with a grin.

Sally was down the steps in a flash. I followed, afraid to go, but more afraid not to stay with her. Mark came more slowly, looking surprised and a little embarrassed when I glared at him.

Sally Rachel stopped on the bottom step and waved the penlight around, trying to see the whole room without going any farther. The space was small, stone lined, and dry. A row of shelves held glass jars full of something black and disgusting looking. Some of them had cracked and the contents were oozing out.

"Let's go back, Sally. That stuff smells awful. There's nothing to see." I felt more and more jittery. A strong sense of sadness washed over me.

"Look!" Sally exclaimed. "Over there."

We looked as she moved the circle of light down the far wall. Lined up neatly on the floor was a row of rotting teddy bears. Six of them, laid out as if for a nap.

Inside the Cellar

"Oh, man!" Mark exclaimed.

Sally Rachel was across the room like a shot. My goosebumps popped out again, and I had a sudden urge to run back into the daylight. Mark pushed forward, leaving me no choice but to go down.

Sally shone the light on each teddy bear in turn. Some still wore shreds of a little vest, or had the remains of a blanket over their legs. All had moldy ribbons tied around their necks.

All but one.

"This bear has on a necklace," Sally Rachel said.

Kneeling beside it, I saw a three-strand necklace shaped like a bib around the bear's crumbling neck. I rubbed the dust off with my finger. It was made of white, blue, red, and black stones carved in the shape of birds, bears, foxes and something that looked like a dog. They were delicate and as smooth as silk.

"Let me *see*, Joanna," Sally Rachel demanded, pushing my hand away. "What are they?"

"I don't know. Some kind of beads. They are beautiful!" I answered.

"Looks like an Indian fetish," Mark said. "We saw some like that in New Mexico last summer. The blue is turquoise, the white is shell, the red is coral, and the black is jet."

"What's a fetish?" Sally Rachel asked

"It's a special charm, I think. I'm not sure exactly what they are used for," Mark explained. "What's it doing here? There haven't been Indians around here in years and years. And why is it on a teddy bear?"

"These teddy bears have been here years and years," Sally Rachel said. "Let's take the necklace home where we can see it better." She reached across me to grab it.

"Wait!" I cried, catching her hand. "The string is probably rotten. It might break if you pull on it. Besides, I'm not sure we should bother it. Looks like the teddy bears were deliberately put here, not just dumped. Why? Who left them?"

8

"Yeah, and why in the cellar instead of in the house?" Mark asked.

"I have a feeling there's something strange behind all this," Sally Rachel said softly.

"You might be right," I agreed. "Why don't we investigate and see if we can find out? Solving a mystery will be something fun to do this summer."

"All you think about is mysteries, Joanna," Sally Rachel pointed out.

Well, mystery stories *are* my favorite thing, but it's really not *all* I think about. Sally Rachel likes to be dramatic.

"Isn't this on Aunt Florrie's land?" Mark asked. "Maybe she knows something about it."

"She might," I said, "but if we tell the grown-ups and it is something interesting, they will take over and it won't be our mystery anymore."

"And if it turns out to be something *they* think is dangerous, they will make us give it up," Sally Rachel added. "I think we should keep it a secret and investigate on our own."

"How can we investigate and keep it secret too? Won't they be just a teeny bit suspicious when we start asking questions about old teddy bears and Indian fetishes we found in a ruined house in the woods?" Mark asked sarcastically.

9

"We won't mention the teddy bears," I said, thinking hard. "We can ask about the history of the area. Who lived here? Why did they leave? They must have left in a hurry to leave their toys behind. Was there a town here then?"

"But if we start asking about it, someone might come out here to see, and find the teddy bears," Sally Rachel objected.

"It was just chance you found that iron ring to the trap door, Sally. We'll cover it up and not tell anyone about the cellar. Mark, you are good with history. You can check the library for information. There has to be a reason why this house is here."

"I guess so," Mark agreed grudgingly. His enthusiasm was not exactly overwhelming. He had been grumpy ever since he and Aunt Laura got here, so I ignored his pouting.

"Then it's settled," I said with a shiver of excitement. "This will be our secret mystery to solve this summer. Deal?"

"Deal," they both replied.

"Sally Rachel, promise you won't tell anyone," I urged.

"I can keep a secret as good as you, Joanna," she snapped. "Let's see if the rest of these teddy bears have anything special."

Thunder rolled overhead as we knelt on

the stone floor in the dark cellar. Sally turned the penlight on the other bears, and we looked closer. They were all alike, as if the same person had made them with only minor differences. There were tatters of a red vest here, a green one there. The eyes, clouded with dust, were made of old-fashioned buttons. The furry, cloth skin was rotted and split, letting the straw stuffing spill out. There was none of the usual warm, cozy teddy bear feeling about them. They made me think of a ritual burial of some kind.

"Let's get out of here," I croaked. Something had happened to my voice. "This place gives me the creeps, and it still stinks."

"Can't we take the necklace?" Sally Rachel pleaded.

"Let's leave it," I said. "For all we know, the owners might have had the plague or something."

"Thanks a lot, Joanna," Sally Rachel said, briskly rubbing her hand on her shorts.

I carefully wiped my fingers across my shirttail. I was beginning to scare myself.

"Shine the light over there, Sal, and let's see the rest of the cellar," Mark said. "There might be a clue somewhere."

"Good idea," she said and swung the light slowly around the room.

In the opposite corner, under the stairs, a child's tea set was scattered across the floor. Under it were shreds of a towel that must have been the tablecloth for a tea party. The little set was made of white china and included a tea pot, sugar bowl, and six tiny cups and saucers. The cups were upset, as though someone had jumped up suddenly and knocked them over.

"Looks like some kids put the bears to bed and then had tea," Mark said dryly.

"Why did they leave in such a hurry?" I murmured to myself, making mental notes. This might be our most important clue.

Besides the tea set and the teddy bears, the only things in the cellar were the smelly jars and a couple of saucers filled with melted candle wax. Except for a thick layer of dust, the cellar was surprisingly clean and free of moisture. But it was a strange place for children to play.

"Okay, let's go," Sally Rachel ordered. She started up the stairs with the flashlight, leaving Mark and me in the dark.

"Hey, wait for us," Mark called, as we scrambled after her.

"Now, let's hide the trap door so no one can see it," Sally Rachel said.

We lowered the heavy door, and scattered

dirt and rubble on top, until it was invisible. Mark sat the broken chair over it. No one would ever notice the trap door was there.

"We better brush the floor so our footprints won't show," Sally Rachel said. "Then nobody could tell we were here."

"Good thinking," I agreed, and began smoothing the dust and dirt back over the floor with a bunch of leaves. Mark spread bits of wood, trash, and sticks around until it looked pretty much the way we found it.

"Tomorrow we'll start asking about the house," Mark said. "I'll check out the local library and see if there's a museum nearby. You girls are better at talking to people than I am. You can do the interviewing."

Mark was beginning to sound excited. When he and Aunt Laura met us in Dallas three days ago, we learned that Uncle Stewart, Mark's dad, had walked out on them. Aunt Laura cried all the time and Mark was angry and bad-tempered. I felt terribly sorry for him, but he was too prickly to let anyone help him. Maybe this would take his mind off his troubles for a while.

The rain had stopped while we were in the cellar. The trees dripped mournfully and the light was still gray and gloomy. As I looked

back to see if we had covered our tracks, I
saw something move at the window. My heart
jumped, and I gasped for air.

There was a nightmare looking in through
the window.

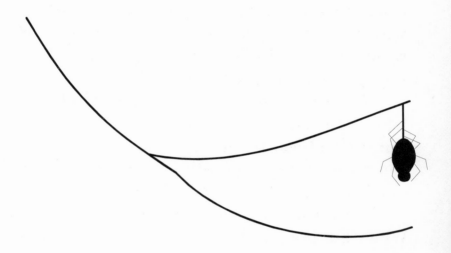

A Witch in the Window

Glittering black eyes glared at us from a gray-white face half hidden under a black hood. A sunken, toothless mouth twisted in a silent snarl. The pointed nose hooked down, almost touching a sharp chin.

I tried to warn the others, but all that came out was a gargled gulp. Mark must have heard because he turned at the same time Sally Rachel called an impatient, "Come *on*, Joanna. Let's go!"

"Oh, man!" Mark said, his voice hoarse and low.

"Joanna, look! It's a witch!" Sally Rachel shrieked as she saw it.

At her cry, the thing disappeared from the window. There was no sound. It was just gone.

We stood frozen, too stunned to move. Mark was the first to recover.

"Come on," he shouted. "Maybe we can still catch it."

He was out the door in a dead run. I wasn't sure I wanted to catch it, but neither did I want us to be separated. I grabbed Sally Rachel's hand and followed right on Mark's heels.

By the time we got to the back of the house, there was nothing there. The wet grass under the window was slightly flattened, but that was all to tell us we weren't losing our minds. The woods were quiet, except for the drip of water off the trees. Nothing moved.

"Joanna, it *was* a witch, wasn't it?" Sally Rachel sounded a little shaky. She hugged my hand tighter.

"Don't be silly," I said as sternly as I could. "There's no witches around here. Probably just an old person out for a walk. We scared her, that's all." It was hard to keep my voice steady. I didn't entirely believe what I was saying.

"Out for a walk in the rain?" Mark asked in disbelief "And how do you know it was a *her?* Could have been a *he*-witch."

"Mark, stop it!" I snarled, suddenly furious

16

with him for speaking my doubts. Putting an arm around Sally Rachel, I said more quietly, "I think it's time we got back to the house. Mom will be wondering where we are."

"I have a feeling it *was* a witch," Sally Rachel mumbled under her breath.

"Nonsense!" I said sharply. "Besides, witches don't look like that anymore. They are modern and up-to-date. Probably look just like us."

I was grasping at anything I could think of to squash the witch idea, as much for my sake as hers. To tell the truth, witches and witchcraft scare me to death. We had a lesson on how to recognize and stay away from cults and the occult in our youth group at church. It was terrifying. I didn't want anything to do with any of it. There had to be another explanation.

It was a silent walk through the rain-soaked forest back to Aunt Florrie's house. When we got there, Mom and Aunt Laura were gone and there was a note on the table. "Come to the shop. We need your help," it commanded.

Aunt Florrie's Yesteryear Antiques shop was at the resort area on the other side of the lake. The "resort" was a pavilion with picnic tables, cabins, RV spaces, a fishing dock, swimming beach, and boat rentals, along with several small shops and boutiques. A post office, grocery store, church, and gas station completed the small vacation village. It was a popular spot for tourists and locals, especially young people, during the summer. The antique shop did a good business.

Aunt Florrie and Uncle Edward built their log house at the far end of the lake in the quiet and privacy of the piney woods. When Uncle Edward died a couple of years ago, Aunt Florrie stayed on to run the shop.

It was about a mile around the lake to the resort, so, after a quick snack, we got our bikes and took the graveled road to the village. None of us talked about the face in the window. We were too shaken up to discuss it, even though I'm sure Sally Rachel and Mark were thinking about it as hard as I was. For the moment, we tried to pretend it hadn't happened.

At Yesteryear Antiques, Mom and Aunt Laura were unpacking boxes of glassware that Aunt Florrie had bought at auction, before she went to the hospital. She specialized in glass items: depression glass, carnival ware, cut glass, old china, mugs, even china dolls. There was shredded paper all over the floor, and the new things sat everywhere.

Mom looked flustered. Aunt Laura's eyes were red from crying. Anger, disgust, and pain flashed in turn across Mark's face.

"Joanna, where have you kids been? We looked everywhere for you!" Mom's voice was sharp.

"We got caught in the thunderstorm and waited in an old house in the woods," I explained. I was the one held responsible for what we did, no matter whose fault or idea it was.

"Joanna is so sensible," Mom liked to brag. "We can depend on her to follow the rules and do the right thing."

I was more comfortable doing what I knew was expected of me, but this statement always made me squirm. Being "sensible" sounded so uninteresting. Sally Rachel nudged me with her elbow when I mentioned the old house.

"I wish you would tell us where you're going. You know how we worry," Mom fussed.

"Sorry," I murmured.

"Now that you're here, give us a hand unpacking these things. We need to get everything sorted and tagged before the weekend crowds come."

Mom was upset, and I didn't think it was only because of us. Between worrying about Aunt Florrie's surgery, Aunt Laura's problems, and running somebody else's store, she was pretty stressed out. Mom was the sensible one in her generation. Aunt Florrie was a romantic. Her head was full of daydreams and the latest book she had read. Everyone was surprised when she turned out to be a pretty good businesswoman. Aunt Laura was flighty and scatterbrained, depending on Uncle Stewart to hold things together. How would she ever manage without him?

Sally and I took a box and began unwrapping the lovely glassware. Aunt Florrie had a good eye for beauty. I loved the soft colors and smooth feel of the old glass. We made separate stacks of pink, green, blue, white, and amethyst dishes. Aunt Laura wiped them with a towel and arranged them on antique tables, and in china closets that were collector's items themselves.

Mark began picking up paper and stuffing it into a garbage bag. His face was red and his jaw stubbornly stiff. He jammed each wad into the plastic bag viciously. I thought any minute he would explode.

I knew he must be hurting over his parents' separation. Sometimes I think he worked up his anger just to keep from crying.

Swinging around carelessly, his elbow caught a crystal vase and sent it crashing to the floor.

"Mark, watch what you're doing!" Aunt

Laura shouted. "We can't afford your careless-ness. Why can't you be more responsible?"

Mark froze, not saying anything. Every muscle in his body tensed. He opened his mouth, snapped it shut, then turned and banged out the door.

Aunt Laura dissolved in sobs and Mom steered her into the back room calling over her shoulder, "Joanna, clean up that mess."

"Get the dustpan, Sally, and let's pick this up," I said with a sigh.

"Why do we have to clean up his messes?" she asked indignantly. "I have a feeling he's go-ing to be a big pain this summer. I wish he hadn't come."

"I know. It's not going to be easy, but we can't get rid of him. I wish Aunt Laura and Uncle Stewart could solve their problems. That's what makes Mark so unhappy. Maybe our mystery will give him something else to think about, and he'll feel better."

"I sure hope so. I can do without a crazy cousin throwing mad fits every second," Sally Rachel declared, rolling her eyes.

We swept up the sparkling bits of glass and were about to tackle the last box of dishes when the bell over the door jingled.

It was late for customers, and I expected an apologetic Mark. It was Mark, but he didn't look very apologetic. He had a "Help

Wanted" sign in his hand and a determined, stubborn look on his face.

"You can run this place without me," he said through clenched teeth. "I've got a job at the picnic pavilion. I'm too clumsy and irresponsible for this work, anyway."

He whirled and slammed out the door again before we could say a word. Mom and Aunt Laura came through the doorway from the back room.

"Mark . . ." Aunt Laura cried tearfully, starting after him.

"Let him go, Laura," Mom said in a calm voice. "It might be better if he works on his own. He has his own problems to sort out."

"I don't blame him for being angry," Aunt Laura sobbed. "It's my fault. And Stewart's. I just hate seeing him so hurt. Maybe it will help if he meets new people."

"Oh, sure," Sally Rachel muttered. "And guess who gets to do his share of the work around here?"

"It won't be that much," I whispered to her. "Besides, Mark will meet different people than we will here. He can ask them about the stone house."

"That's true," she admitted, her eyes flashing. "Let's hurry and finish, so we can start investigating."

Where is Mark?

The weekend was on us, and there was no time to think about the stone house and the horrible thing in the window. The shop was filled with customers from the time it opened at 9:00 A.M. until it closed at 6:00. Sally Rachel and I waited on people, helped refill tables and shelves from supplies in the back room, and tried to keep the shop neat. Mom and Aunt Laura took care of the cash register and any information a customer might want on a particular item.

Sally Rachel was better than I at waiting on customers. She liked people. Her wide-eyed innocence and pretty smile charmed them into buying things they didn't even know they wanted. She didn't have much staying power, though. She was always running out for a Coke, or to visit with Mark at the pavilion.

Mark left the house right after breakfast, and didn't come back until supper time. I hoped he was having more luck finding out about the stone house that Sally and I were. Most of the weekend people who came into the shop were out-of-towners. They knew less than we did about the history of the area.

Sundays we opened at noon. By 2:30 the place was jammed. The lake was crowded with boats, and the pavilion overflowed with swimmers and picnickers. Stopping for a minute to rest and get a drink, I watched the crowd filter in and out. They were the usual tourist types: sunburned, windblown, mostly in t-shirts and shorts. Some came especially for the antiques. Others drifted in from the picnic grounds and lake "just to look."

One neatly dressed, dignified, old lady stood out among the sloppy shoppers. Her blue dress looked expensive and her thick white hair was smoothed into a bun on her neck. I caught her watching me with a curiously suspicious look. Her eyes were as black as night.

My first thought was, *Where have I seen her before?* Then she smiled, a friendly smile that made her eyes twinkle and look much too young for the wrinkled face.

Sally Rachel came to me with a puzzled

look. "Joanna, do you see that lady in the blue dress?" she asked. "Does she look familiar to you?"

"At first I thought I had seen her somewhere, but now I don't think so," I said, watching her browse around the room. "I suppose she just reminds us of someone."

"I guess so," Sally agreed. "I hope during the week there's fewer people and more buyers."

We were catching on fast to the business of retail selling. More people didn't necessarily mean more sales. Personally, I liked the crowded days because people didn't have time to chat. When they did, sooner or later someone came up with the question I dreaded most.

"Is your older daughter adopted?" they would ask Mom in a low voice they thought I couldn't hear. My tall, skinny figure, with awkward, knobby knees and elbows, and my unmanageable red hair were quite a contrast to Mom and Sally Rachel's graceful, curvy bodies and blond curls.

This was usually followed quickly by how "nice" is was to be "chosen" for a family, until Mom could break in and say with pride, "No, Joanna takes after her great-grandmother on her father's side."

I never knew Great Grandma Louisa. In spite of the stories Granny and Dad often told about what a fascinating person she was, and how lucky I was to be like her, I still felt like an outsider in my family. Even Dad was blond and blue-eyed, with no trace of the red hair gene.

"There is only one redhead in every third or fourth generation," they said.

I was a "throwback" and it wasn't very comfortable. I bet Great Grandma Louisa didn't like looking different either. I wonder if she smiled and pretended she didn't hear, or that it didn't matter, the way I do?

I reminded myself that I was going to have to talk to people to find out what happened at the stone house. But that's different. In solving a mystery, you're gathering evidence, not just chatting. I let Sally Rachel do most of the talking. She can wheedle things out of anybody.

Monday and Tuesday were practically dead. The few people we talked to knew nothing about East Texas history. On Wednesday Mom told us we could have the morning off, and Sally Rachel and I decided to take another look at the ruined house. We were reluctant to go without Mark, but our curiosity was bigger than our fear.

"We should take a different way each time, so we don't make a path," Sally observed. "We don't want anybody to know where we're going."

"Right," I said. It was irritating how often she was right. I should have thought of that. I was the mystery specialist.

The woods were cheerful with happy bird and squirrel chatter in the tree tops. The sun was warm. The shadows were inviting and friendly. Our fears were gone by the time we reached the clearing.

Sunlight streamed through the trees, bathing the stone house in a golden glow. It didn't look as scary as before. It was just an old house, broken, and battered and very sad.

"Wait," I whispered, stopping behind a tree. "We have to check it out before we rush in." My mystery-solving instincts were working again.

Sally rolled her eyes in her "Oh, good heavens!" look, but she stopped and we stood silently watching. Everything looked normal and peaceful.

"Okay, let's go," I said, stepping into the open.

"Joanna, wait. I have a feeling . . . what's that noise?"

I heard it as she spoke. A low, moaning sound came from the house. It hummed in the air and began to climb higher, getting louder

27

as it rose. It swelled and grew into an ear-splitting shriek, then trailed off in a cackling laugh, followed by total silence.

Panic took over. We ran, crashing through the woods, not minding the noise we made or the scratches we collected. Halfway home, we stumbled to a stop, gasping for breath.

"Joanna, what was it?" Sally Rachel wheezed. "Is it the witch, or is it haunted?"

"I don't know," I admitted, puffing and choking. "Maybe it *is* haunted. I don't think even a witch would sound like that."

"If it's haunted, how are we going to get back in to see about the teddy bears? And the necklace! Joanna, we have to get the necklace! If it's a witch, she might steal it."

"Witches don't have to steal. They put spells on things. Anyway, there's no such thing as a witch," I said, still panting. I didn't know any rules that covered something like this. What was I supposed to do now?

"I have a feeling — "

"Enough of your *feelings*," I snapped. "Let's go home. We'll tell Mark about it. Maybe he'll know what to do."

"Okay," Sally said quietly. With a sweet, trusting smile, she took my hand.

"Sorry I barked at you," I mumbled, squeezing her hand. "I guess I was really scared."

"Me too," she admitted.

We walked hand in hand the rest of the way to the house, each wrapped in our own thoughts. I had never heard such a horrible sound. Just thinking about it sent cold chills down my back. Sally Rachel was right. We should get the necklace out of the cellar. And maybe one of the teddy bears. We might have to prove what we found there.

Maybe Mark had found out something about the place. After supper we would tell him what happened, and see if he had any suggestions.

That afternoon in the shop, Sally Rachel and I were jumpy and distracted, and Mom fussed at us more than once. We were bursting with the need to talk about what had happened. I slipped over to the pavilion on a break, but Mark was cleaning out boats and couldn't stop. Somehow, we managed to make it 'til 6:00.

Mark was not home by supper time, so we ate without him. "Looks like he could let us know when he has to work late," Aunt Laura complained. "He doesn't seem to have any sense of responsibility anymore."

"Maybe he's too busy to call. They're having a dance there Friday night. There's lots to get done by then . . ." I explained.

"I have a feeling he's probably talking to a girl," Sally Rachel said. "He was checking out one of the waitresses in the restaurant yesterday."

"I hope that's all it is," Aunt Laura said with a sigh.

"I wouldn't worry about Mark," Mom said calmly. "He's a very capable person, and it's pretty quiet around here. If there had been an accident, someone would have called. He'll have a good reason for being late when he gets home."

After supper, when the kitchen chores were done, Sally Rachel and I wandered restlessly into the living room.

"Sally, let's learn this game," I said, finding an old deck of Rook cards in the desk. I had to do something. My jitters were growing.

"I don't like card games, Joanna," she complained.

"Come on, it looks interesting. It'll help pass the time."

"Okay, if it's not too hard," she agreed grumpily.

Sally Rachel caught on to the game fast, and was soon holding her own. We sprawled on the living room rug, absorbed in the cards. The comfortable hum of Mom's and Aunt Laura's voices from the kitchen was soothing, and we forgot our fright for a while. Now and then I'd catch a word or phrase of their conversation.

"... beautiful silver jewelry ... from New Mexico, I think ... not quite right for Florrie's shop ... hear about the robberies ... might be a pickpocket ..."

The little clock on the mantle struck ten times. Mark was still not home.

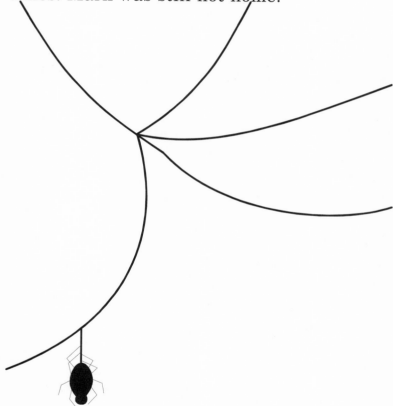

An
Accident and an Intruder

Suddenly, the comforting hum from the kitchen changed. There was a sharp, "Oh, no!" and Aunt Laura hurried in, her face white and frightened.

"I called the pavilion. The night guard said Mark left around eight o'clock. It only takes fifteen minutes to get home on his bike. Something's happened! We have to find him!" she cried. Her voice was high and scratchy with alarm.

"Calm down, Laura," Mom soothed. "I'll get the car and we'll drive over there. If he's had an accident on the way home we'll find him. Perhaps he's just visiting with friends and forgot the time."

"Sally Rachel said he was flirting with a

waitress," I reminded them. "Maybe she flirted back."

That didn't get the smiles I hoped it would. Even Sally looked worried, her eyes dark and scared. I could see an "I have a feeling . . ." coming on.

I grabbed a big flashlight from the hall table and we piled into the car.

Mom drove slowly with the headlights on bright. I leaned out the back window and waved the flashlight beam down the side of the road. We were a little over halfway when we saw him. Aunt Laura and I were out of the car before it stopped, running to the crumpled shape at the foot of a tree. The bicycle lay in a heap, the front wheel twisted and bent.

"Mark! Mark, are you all right?" Aunt Laura cried, lifting his head gently. She gasped as her hands came away sticky with blood. "He's hurt, Joanna! We have to get him to a doctor!"

I turned the flashlight directly on his face. There was so much blood, it was hard to tell where he was hurt. His eyelids fluttered and he moaned.

"Mark, can you hear me?" I asked, taking his hand.

"Joanna?" he murmured thickly, then as his eyes came open, "Mom, I'm glad you found me."

"Mark, what happened? Did a car run you off the road?" Mom asked, kneeling beside us.

"Something's wrong with my bike," he said slowly. "The wheel came loose. I was hurrying because I was late and I couldn't control it."

"How long have you been lying here?" Aunt Laura asked, her voice jerky with fear. She tried to clean some of the blood from his face with a tissue. There appeared to be a gash on his forehead and a long scrape on his cheek.

"Awhile," he said faintly. "I tried to walk home, but I got dizzy and passed out when I stood up. Oh, man, my head hurts!"

"Can you stand if we help you?" she asked again. "You need a doctor for that cut on your head."

With the three of us helping him, Mark struggled to his feet. We eased him into the back seat between Aunt Laura and me. Sally Rachel sat in front, oddly silent. Mom rushed us to the emergency room in Kennard, about ten minutes away.

The doctor on duty put four stitches in Mark's forehead and a dressing on his cheek.

"Face wounds bleed a lot," he explained. "They often look worse than they are. He has a mild concussion, but with a little rest he should be fine."

As soon as we got home, Mark took something for his headache. Then Mom and Aunt Laura put him straight to bed. It was very late, and the excitement of the day had drained us.

I heard Sally Rachel whisper, just as I was dropping off to sleep, "Joanna, I'm scared. I have a feeling Mark's accident wasn't just an accident. He is so picky about that bicycle. It's in perfect shape. I don't think I like what's happening."

"Neither do I," I murmured, too near sleep to tackle the problem. "We'll talk about it in the morning."

Next morning, Mark was much better except for a headache. When Aunt Laura called his boss and explained what happened, he gave Mark a couple of days off to recuperate. Mom asked Sally and me to stay with him. When she and Aunt Laura left for the shop, we had the day to ourselves.

"Mark, we have so much to tell you," Sally Rachel babbled, too excited to hold it any longer.

"What?" Mark asked, frowning. His morning aspirin obviously wasn't working yet.

"Joanna and I went back to the stone house yesterday, and the scariest noise came out of it. It sounded like a ghost howling."

"Yeah?" Mark scoffed, his eyes closed. "You sure it wasn't your witch chanting a spell?"

"It's true, Mark," I said quickly. "It was really terrible. I've never heard anything so awful. We didn't wait to investigate."

His eyes cracked open to a slit. "You're serious, aren't you?" he exclaimed, finally paying attention. "What's going on around here? Howling in the woods and sabotage at the lake. Threats too. There was a note tied to my bike handlebars saying "mind your own business." I thought one of the guys at work was playing a joke and threw it away. But someone deliberately messed with my bike. I know it was okay yesterday morning. I've got to go get it and take a look."

"We'll get it for you," I insisted, as he staggered and clutched his head. "You wait right here. Come on, Sally."

The bicycle was still under the tree where we left it. When we picked it up, its front wheel dangled out of the frame. The spokes were broken and bent. Half carrying, half rolling, we managed to get it to the house. When Mark examined it and found a bolt missing from the front wheel, he was furious.

"Oh, man, this bike was brand new! My dad gave it to me. I'm going to find out who did this!"

"I wonder if this has anything to do with the stone house?" Sally Rachel asked. "Is that what the note meant? Maybe someone doesn't want us to find out why the teddy bears are there." Her voice dropped to an eerie pitch, and her narrowed eyes slid from side to side. "Something terrible might have happened, and they don't want anybody to know it."

"Mark, have you asked anyone about the house? Sally and I haven't found out a thing," I said, ignoring her theatrics.

"I didn't ask specifically about the house, but I did find out a few things about this area. A long time ago, there used to be a sawmill here. The lake was the mill pond. Little towns grew around the mills, and then disappeared when the mill closed," he explained crossly. "How would anyone know we are interested in the house? Why would they care?"

"The thing we saw in the window knows," Sally Rachel suggested darkly. "Maybe it's her house and she's trying to scare us off. We have to go back and get the necklace, Joanna, before something happens to it."

I was hoping she had forgotten about that. Grudgingly, I had to admit it made sense. Without the necklace, or one of the bears, we couldn't prove anything had been there. If Mark's accident was connected in some way with the house, we might need proof more than ever.

"Mark ... did you tell anyone why we want to know about the house?" I asked.

"Only Lester," he mumbled.

"Who's Lester?" Sally Rachel asked.

"A guy who works at the pavilion. He's my friend."

"Would he have any reason to not want us near the stone house?" I asked.

"No way. He's summer help like we are. He didn't even know there was a house there until I told him. I didn't mention the teddy bears or what we were doing."

"You *told* him about the house?" I shouted. "Are you sure you didn't tell him about the cellar?"

"'Course I'm sure," he growled. "Don't pick on Les, okay? His dad walked out like mine did. He knows how I feel and he's my friend. We talk. Why don't you just run along and leave me alone? I have to try and fix my bike." His growl had risen to a yell.

"Mark ..." I began, then decided there was no use arguing. "Okay. Sally, let's go. Mr. Wonderful can do without us for a while."

We stalked out, and in silent agreement headed for the path to the clearing. Now was as good a time as any to go get the necklace. I was angry enough with Mark to not think about being afraid.

I hurried through the woods before my courage gave out, paying no attention to Sally Rachel's demands to slow down. Like yesterday, it was sunny and peaceful. The only sounds were normal outdoor noises. After a few minutes of listening, we tiptoed to the empty doorway. All was quiet. We stepped cautiously into the sun-speckled ruins, crossed the front room, and went into the kitchen.

"Joanna, look!" Sally Rachel gasped "Somebody's been here!"

She was right. The floor was scuffed and tracked, and bits of the vines were scattered everywhere. The table lay on its side in the middle of the room. The chair Mark put over the trap door was tossed aside. The trap door was brushed clear of dirt, the iron ring wiped clean. A rusty, iron poker lay next to it, and the heavy door was chipped and pitted at the edges.

Sally Rachel whispered, "Somebody's come to get the teddy bears. Somebody who knows where they are."

Dance with Disaster

Chills shivered up my back.

"We've got to see if the teddy bears and necklace are still there," Sally Rachel insisted. "What if she's already taken them?"

"It doesn't look like whoever it was got the door open," I said, examining the scratches. "I'm not sure we can, either. It was all we could do with Mark's help. And how do you know it was a *she?*" If Sally was referring to the witch again, I was still not buying it.

"It has to be the witch. We've got to try, Joanna. I have a feeling this might be our last chance."

"Okay, we'll try," I agreed reluctantly. "You take that poker and stick it under the edge when I lift the door."

I braced my feet and pulled the iron ring with all my strength. The door moved about half an inch. Not enough to slide the poker under it.

"Come on, Joanna. Pull!" Sally demanded.

"I'm trying," I puffed. Grasping the ring again, I pulled until my arms felt like they would be yanked from their sockets. It was still not enough.

"We have to wait until Mark can help us," I gasped, collapsing on the floor. "We can't do it by ourselves."

"Let's go get him. Hurry!" She grabbed my hand to pull me up.

"Mark's been hurt. He can't do this now," I protested.

"He has to! We have to see if the teddy bears are still there. She knows where they are," Sally insisted.

I was beginning to wish I hadn't suggested we solve the mystery of the teddy bears. Sally Rachel was getting too carried away. She always got excited about whatever her current thing was, but I had never seen her this upset. The teddy bears were taking on an importance I wasn't sure they deserved.

"Maybe she, or whoever, was just curious about what's under the door, like we were," I said, trying to calm her down. It didn't work.

"Please, Joanna. Let's go home and get Mark," Sally begged.

"Okay. We'll go home and tell Mark what we've found, and see what he says," I compromised.

Sally Rachel took off at a trot, and this time I hurried to keep up with her. We hadn't gone far when we saw Mark coming in our direction.

"Mark! How's your head? You have to come and help us if it's better," Sally spluttered.

"My head is better. My bike's a mess. Wait'll I catch up with whoever did this!" he scowled, shaking his fist. He looked a little pale, but free of pain.

"Someone has been in the stone house trying to open the trap door. Sally Rachel feels we have to see if they bothered the teddy bears," I explained.

"And the necklace! Remember the necklace," she reminded us, her eyes sparkling with excitement. "Joanna and I can't open the trap door by ourselves. You have to help us."

"I'm not sure I'm up to lifting stones, Sal. Can't it wait a day or two?" he asked.

"No, it can't!" she cried. "I have a feeling we have to do it right now!"

"Oh, man, deliver us from your feelings," Mark groaned. "All right. We'll give it a try."

"Mark, don't you think . . ." I started, but cut it off when his slow wink told me not to worry.

The clearing was still peaceful and Sally Rachel ran into the house without hesitation. With Mark's help, we lifted the stone door and propped it open. Sally pulled the little penlight from her pocket and hurried down the stairs.

The teddy bears were exactly as we had left them. Nothing had been disturbed.

"Joanna, get the bear with the necklace," Sally directed.

I knelt on the cold floor and tried to pick it up. It fell apart into a heap of straw.

"It's too rotted to pick up," I said, gently laying it back. "We'll just take the necklace." I carefully unwound the necklace from the straw, and slipped it into my pocket.

"Let's go before whoever was here comes back," I urged, anxious to be out of the creepy cellar.

We closed the trap door, not trying to hide it again. As we left the clearing, I had a prickly feeling someone was watching. I stopped and looked back, but no one was there. The birds sang, the squirrels chattered, the sun danced through the trees in a perfectly normal way. Even so, I ran to catch up with the others as though demons were after me.

Back at the house, I spread the necklace on the kitchen table and cleaned it with a damp paper towel. Its string was brittle and thin, but the beautifully carved figures glowed. The jet black beads set off the colors of the red, turquoise, and white ones.

Each little figure was carefully made and polished smooth as glass. There were birds with folded wings, chunky bears, skinny foxes with delicate, pointed ears. The fourth figure, Mark said, was a coyote.

"It took someone a long time to make these. It must be pretty valuable," he said, his voice full of admiration.

We put it in a plastic sandwich bag, and Sally Rachel tucked it under her t-shirts in the dresser drawer, making sure we knew where it was.

Mark went to bed with another aspirin. Sally and I rode over to the shop. The crowd was thin but steady, and we had a chance to ask a few questions about local history. Only one grizzled, old man who wandered in from the heat knew anything helpful.

"Seems I recollect something about a town being here," he said, pleased that we would chat with him. He shut his eyes for a moment then snapped his fingers. "Yep, there was.

When I was just knee-high to a grasshopper, my dad told me about the time the sawmill was here. A regular town it was then. Lots of houses all over these woods."

"Were they made out of stone?" Sally Rachel asked.

"Mostly out of lumber from the mill. I believe he did mention a house made of stone. It was out in the woods by itself. When the mill shut down, all the people left. I don't reckon anyone has thought about that old house since."

"Do you know who built it?" I asked casually.

"No, don't reckon I do," he mumbled.

"What happened to the mill?" I asked.

"Don't recall," he said. "Sometimes they just ran out of trees and quit. Sometimes an accident shut them down. They had lots of accidents. Now and then it was deliberate mischief. Uh-oh, here comes the missus. Nice visiting with you." He scurried after a plump lady peering in the door before we could say thanks.

Interesting, I thought. If the mill had simply run out of trees, everyone would have had time to pack up and move. The teddy bears would never have been left in the cellar. Why was the stone house off by itself? The child, or children, who lived there must have had friends. I couldn't imagine one child having six teddy bears all alike. Remembering the sadness of the ruins, I wondered if some tragedy had happened there. Maybe it was better if we didn't find out.

Late the next morning, Mark went back to work to help get ready for the dance that night. It was for junior and senior high kids, and Mom promised I could go. Sally Rachel wasn't happy about being left out.

She watched grimly as the dock and pavilion were strung with colored lanterns. A local disc jockey would supply the music, and the resort was offering free soft drinks and chips.

"It's not fair," she muttered. "I'm supposed to do everything else you do, but I can't go to the dance. It's not fair!"

"I agree," I soothed. "Don't worry. It won't be long before you are old enough to go to dances."

"If I live that long," she grumbled.

Mom did my hair in a thick French braid and tied it with a green ribbon. I knew it wouldn't be long before it was all frizzy again around my face, but for once it looked pretty decent. A full-skirted green and white dress hid my sharp angles. And excitement, instead of chills, shivered through me.

Under the soft glow of the lanterns, Mark looked quite dashing with the bandage on his forehead and the long scratch down his cheek.

He was never without a girl or two hanging on every word of a story that got better each time it was told. The dark-haired waitress Sally Rachel had mentioned stuck to Mark like glue. She was little and cute with silky curls. She had a perfect figure and dimples. Her adoring glances at Mark were definitely overdone. Mark blushed and smiled, and loved every minute of it.

To my surprise, some of the attention spilled over on me. I was asked to tell how we waited and worried, and how we finally found Mark under the tree. Until the novelty of the accident wore off, I would have plenty of dance partners.

One of them was Mark's friend, Lester Murray.

"Hello-o-o, Joanna," he said when Mark introduced us. "Mark's told me a lot about you." His eyes slid over me in a way that made me uncomfortable.

"Hi," I said, shrinking a little from his outstretched hand. I didn't like him. I couldn't say why, but he instantly turned me off.

Lester was older than most of the others and sort of good looking with short, curly blond hair, blue eyes and sharp features — the kind the movie ads call "chiseled." He had a nice smile and plenty of charm. Slightly taller than I, he was an expert dancer and I enjoyed the dancing, in spite of my feelings.

The music was loud and jazzy. The crowd was cool and the night was balmy. I was having a wonderful time. It got even better when the next guy to cut in was tall, red-haired and lanky like me. After looking over the heads, or eyeball to eyeball with most of the boys, it felt strange and nice to look up to one.

"Hi, Joanna, I'm Rusty Carter," he said. "Looks like you and me could have come out of the same pod."

I didn't know what to do with that line, so I laughed and asked breezily, "Is Rusty really your name, or is it a nickname?"

"I was christened Sebastian. My mother is a romantic," he said, rolling his eyes much like Sally Rachel. "Everyone calls me Rusty."

"I think I like your mother," I said, smiling at him. "Sebastian is a neat name, but I'll call you Rusty, if you prefer."

"Thanks," he replied.

He had a nice grin that enhanced his eyes. We swept into the next dance, and the next, and the one after that. Rusty had a way of refusing to let anyone cut in that made me feel tingly and special. For a while, I forgot about rotting teddy bears, stone houses, witches, and accidents that might not be accidents.

About 9:30, I noticed that Mark looked pale and quiet.

"Do you want to go home?" I asked. "I'll call Mom."

I knew his head must be hurting when he agreed without an argument.

Mom wasn't expecting to come for us until 11:00. Since Mark's accident, she wouldn't let us go out at night by ourselves.

"Mom, Mark isn't feeling well. Can you come after us?" I asked.

"Uh . . . oh, Joanna. Yes, I'll be there in a few minutes," she stammered with a sniff.

"Mom? What's wrong? Are you crying?" I was instantly jerked off my cloud. My calm, steady mother almost never cried.

"It's Sally Rachel," she said between sniffs. "She fell in the lake and almost drowned. She insists she was pushed."

The Witch Strikes Again

I t was Aunt Laura who came for us.

"What happened?" I demanded as soon as the car stopped.

"We're not sure," she said. "Sally Rachel was by the lake in front of the house. We heard a scream, and found her in the water holding on to a tree root. I know she wouldn't have deliberately jumped in because she can't swim. She says someone pushed her, but we didn't see anyone. She was scared to death, but she won't, or can't, tell us who it was."

"Oh, man," Mark whispered hoarsely.

When we got home, Sally Rachel was huddled in her bathrobe, wet hair curling around her face, her eyes as big as saucers. Mom was kneeling in front of her.

"Joanna, maybe you can get Sally to tell us what happened out there," she said with a teary frown. "I think we ought to call the police."

Sally stared at me, her eyes full of secrets. She gave a tiny shake of her head when Mom mentioned the police.

"Mom, can you make some cocoa? I think it might help calm her down. Mark and I could use some too." I wanted to talk to Sally Rachel in private.

Mom caught on. She wiped her eyes and got to her feet. "Good idea. Laura, come help me. I don't know why I didn't think of cocoa."

As soon as the door closed behind them, Sally Rachel grabbed my hand.

"Joanna, it was the witch! She pushed me in the lake!" Her voice was hardly above a whisper, high-pitched and frantic.

"Are you positive, Sally?" I asked as calmly as I could.

"I saw her, Joanna! She wore a long, black thing and she flapped at me like a big bat. Her hair was frizzed out all over and she looked crazy."

"What were you doing at the lake?" I asked, trying to understand the impossible.

"I was watching the frogs eat supper," she snapped. For Sally Rachel, it was a reasonable answer. "What difference does that

52

make? I was nearly drowned! The witch pushed me in the lake!"

"Come on, Sally, how could she push you if her arms were flapping like bat wings?" Mark pointed out. "Did you actually feel her hands push you? Think carefully. It might be important."

Sally Rachel closed her eyes and wrinkled her forehead. "I was on the edge of the lake by that big tree, where the bank is so steep. I heard something behind me. When I turned around, there she was. She was holding that black thing out, and making that awful moaning sound we heard at the stone house. She was real close, and I stepped back, and . . . and . . ." she faltered.

"And fell over the bank," I finished. "I'm sure it seemed like she pushed you, but I don't think she touched you at all. She was gone by the time Mom got to you. Are you *sure* it was a woman?"

"It's a witch!" Sally insisted. "Witches can push people without touching them, and who else can appear and disappear so fast?"

I had to admit she might have a point. Did this have anything to do with what happened to Mark?

"Could she have left the note on your bike, Mark?" I asked. "And if it *was* her we saw at the window, could the teddy bears be the *busi-*

ness the note warned us to stay out of? Was she watching the whole time we were in the cellar?"

"This is getting too weird for me," Mark said. "Who ever heard of teddy bears being dangerous? I'm going to bed. My head hurts. Glad you're okay, Sal."

"Sally, I think we should tell Mom what's going on, and call the police. It is getting dangerous. You could have drowned! Maybe it's time we dropped the investigation."

"Hot chocolate coming up," Mom called, carrying a tray of steaming mugs from the kitchen. Sally Rachel and I sipped silently until Mom impatiently asked, "Sally, did you tell Joanna what happened?"

"She said a noise scared her, and when she turned around she saw something behind her. It moved, and she stepped back and fell over the bank into the lake," I volunteered.

Sally Rachel shot me a grateful look. It was true as far as it went.

Mom knew Sally Rachel did not make up tales. Her frown deepened.

"What did you see?" she asked gently. "Was it a person or an animal?"

"I'm not sure. It scared me." Sally murmured, forced to tell a half-truth. Lying to Mom made us both uncomfortable.

54

"I think you should stay away from the lake and woods at night," Mom advised. "The world is full of crazy people these days. There might be one or two hiding in these woods."

If you only knew, I thought.

"I'm going to bed," I said with a fake yawn. "Come on, Sally. Let's get some sleep. Things will look better in the morning."

Sally Rachel dropped off at once, but not even the cocoa could help me sleep. Too much had happened that night. First, the wonderful time at the dance when I actually felt attractive and special. Next, Rusty Carter with his friendly grin and his romantic other name, Sebastian. And then the shock of Sally Rachel's accident. Sally who had said "if I live that long" just hours earlier. Had she had a feeling then that something was going to happen?

When I finally slept, my dreams were haunted with grinning teddy bears, enormous bats with witches' faces, and red-haired knights on bicycles who came to rescue me.

The next morning, Dad called to say he was coming next weekend. I was relieved. Dad would understand, and help us sort things out without demanding we drop the whole thing, the way Mom would.

"Wish *my* Dad would come," Mark muttered under his breath. "He could help fix my bike. Grown-ups can act so stupid!"

Aunt Laura heard and turned away, her face stiff. I wondered if she, too, wished Uncle Stewart would come.

The next few days, things were pretty normal. Mark went to work at the pavilion, Sally Rachel and I to Yesteryear Antiques. Business was steady enough to keep us pleasantly busy. Neither Sally nor I asked any more questions about the stone house. I think at that moment we were afraid to know the answers.

Mark, however, was still angry about the damage to his bike. He questioned everyone at the pavilion. The little he learned only added to the puzzle.

"They all swear they didn't do it, and they haven't noticed anyone in particular hanging around the bike rack," he reported one night after supper. "The only person they saw more than once was an old lady who's staying in one of the cabins. Lester says she often sits on the bench by the rack. Probably a tourist on vacation."

"Why would she come *here* for a vacation?" Sally Rachel asked with a little sneer.

"What else does Lester say?" I asked. I know I sounded slightly sarcastic, but I couldn't help it. Mark shot me a warning look.

"He says he'll keep an eye out, and let me know if he sees anything suspicious."

"Mark! How could you tell him our secret?" Sally Rachel said angrily.

"Don't worry. We can trust Les. He's my friend."

I had never seen Mark take to anybody the way he had to Lester Murray. Lester was a good listener, and Mark needed a listener right now who would understand his problem. But Lester made me uneasy, in spite of his obvious charm. The way he looked at me at the dance was embarrassing.

"Well, there isn't any business of Lester's that we are interested in, so he wouldn't have a reason to leave a threatening note or sabotage Mark's bike." Another black look from Mark. "And I don't believe any old lady had anything to do with it, either," I said after thinking it over.

"The witch is old," Sally Rachel said quietly.

"If anyone had seen the face we saw, they would remember it. The news would be all over the place by now," Mark observed.

"I have a feeling she can look any way she likes," Sally persisted.

I wished for the hundredth time I could wipe out the idea of a witch, but evidence was piling up against me. We had all seen the horrible face at the window of the stone house. Sally Rachel had seen it again the night of the dance. Had a "witch" really tried to push her in the lake? Did she know Sally couldn't swim? Did the same "witch" write the note, and fix Mark's bike so the wheel would come off?

The questions whirled in my head. Even after the house was quiet and everyone was asleep, they haunted me. I sat by the window trying to make sense of it all. The face in the window, Mark's bicycle deliberately tampered with, Sally Rachel scared so badly she falls in the lake.

Were all these things connected? Were the "accidents" deliberately planned? Why? We didn't know anyone well enough to cause that kind of dislike or revenge. The only connecting link seemed to be this "witch" person. She turned up at the stone house and, according to Sally Rachel, at the lake.

We did take the necklace from the cellar, but it had been there for ages. Who would care after all these years? How did the teddy bears figure in? Why were they left there?

The scene from my window should have calmed me down. It was a gorgeous night. The moon was full and bright, making silvery-white places next to inky black ones. The air was soft, and smelled like pine needles. I was beginning to relax, when one of the inky spots seemed to move. Instantly wide awake, I looked again.

There was a wedge of shadow in the edge of the trees that looked solid, but not like a tree or a person. As I watched, it glided into the moonlight. Roughly shaped like a triangle, it stopped, and appeared to be staring at the house.

The thing looked unreal until it swung around and slid into the trees. Then I knew. It was a person in a long cape with a hood. The face in the window of the stone house was wearing a hood. The person Sally Rachel had seen at the lake wore a cape. It was her! It had to be!

The shadow stopped just inside the trees, and turned again, as if still watching the house. Without stopping to think, I pulled jeans over my pajamas, pushed my feet into sneakers, and slipped quietly out of the house.

Midnight Shadow

The shadow had disappeared by the time I got to the edge of the woods. I headed cautiously in the direction I thought it took, trying to pick up a trail. The moonlight made open spaces as bright as day, but left the dark patches pitch black and confusing.

Just when I thought I'd lost it, the shadow flowed into the moonlight. It drifted without a sound, as if it didn't quite touch the ground. I shivered in the warm night air.

I tiptoed from tree to tree, concentrating on keeping the thing in sight as it wove in and out of moonlight and darkness. I got the creepy feeling it wasn't a person after all. No human could walk like that. Was I seeing a ghost? That thought was as scary as Sally Rachel's "witch."

Going slowly, it stopped often. It was headed in the direction of the stone house.

A twig snapped in the woods. I looked away for a second, and the thing was gone. I stopped in the shadow of a tree and waited. Nothing moved in the black and white woods. After a minute or two, I tiptoed on, then waited again.

Still nothing.

The empty silence was almost worse than any ghost or witch. It reminded me how alone I was. *This is stupid, Joanna*, I scolded myself. *What are you going to do if it tries to stop you?*

Without thinking, I had given into the urge to follow the shadow. Now I wasn't sure it was a good idea. I ought to turn around and go straight home.

Instead, I followed another impulse. The stone house was close, and I decided to take a quick look. If somebody was going there in the middle of the night, it might be the person who was warning us off.

Leaving the shadow of the tree, I hurried toward the clearing. I hadn't gone ten steps when something snapped against my ankle, throwing me suddenly to the ground. My hands flew out to break the fall, the left one doubling under as my weight come down on it. There was a sharp flash of pain, and darkness closed over my head.

The next thing I knew was a strange, unnatural humming around me. The sound was low, something between a moan and a wail. The notes slid up and down in a monotonous tune. There was a pattering sound, and from my dirt-level view, I saw feet in soft-soled shoes stepping past my nose in a measured rhythm.

I raised my head, and instantly the sound stopped. The feet disappeared. There was a flick of black cloth, and whatever was there was gone.

My wrist and ankle throbbed. My head buzzed. Closing my eyes, I waited a minute, then slowly sat up. My head whirled in dizzy circles. Did I really hear that strange sound? Were there really feet dancing around my head? Surely I imagined it.

A couple of deep breaths cleared my head, and I took stock. My ankle was bruised, but it worked. My wrist was already swelling, and it hurt terribly to move it.

Great, Joanna! I thought. *Just great. Now you've broken your arm!*

Giving in to my impulses was never a good

idea. Why couldn't I remember that? It was always better to follow the rules. After all, rules were made for a good reason. And the new rule was that we were to stay away from the woods at night. Or was it the lake? If only I didn't feel so woozy!

I looked around carefully. The woods were still. There was no lurking shadow that didn't belong there. All the same, I felt a great need to get out of there.

Tucking my throbbing arm into my pajama shirt, Napoleon fashion, I started home. The ankle was stiff and sore, but it held me. I didn't try to be quiet. I just hurried as best I could.

How am I going to explain this? I thought. *Everybody will be furious with me for coming out by myself. Mom will certainly put a stop to everything when she finds out I was chasing ghosts in the middle of the night.*

I stumbled for what seemed like miles before the house came in sight. Several times I stopped and looked back. I couldn't shake the feeling that someone was following me. The impression was strong but, curiously, I didn't feel threatened. Even so, I hobbled faster.

There were lights on at the house. I both dreaded and welcomed the fact that someone was up. My arm needed attention, but I didn't know yet how to explain what had happened.

Stick to the truth as much as you can, Joanna, I reminded myself. But I wasn't sure what was truth. What I thought happened was too fantastic to be true.

I didn't have time to worry about it. *Everybody* was up, and they fell on me when I opened the door. I cried out in pain as Sally Rachel squeezed against my sore arm.

"Joanna, you're hurt!" she yelped. "What happened? Where did you go? Why did you go out without us?"

Questions poured out of all of them as Mom eased me into a chair.

"Your ankle is just bruised," she said after a careful look. "I think your wrist is sprained, but we'll have to have it x-rayed in the morning. I'll get something to wrap it with."

Aunt Laura had gone to the kitchen for ice, and when Mom left the room Sally Rachel knelt by my chair.

"I woke up and you were gone. Did you see the witch too?" she whispered.

I didn't know how to answer her. In spite of everything, I was still not ready to admit to a witch. Mom saved me by coming back in with a roll of elastic bandage, which she wrapped firmly around my hand and wrist. Aunt Laura brought a plastic bag filled with crushed ice wrapped with a towel. She laid it gently on my arm.

"What were you doing outside this time of night?" Mom asked in her "I-want-no-nonsense" tone of voice.

"I couldn't sleep, and I thought I saw someone watching the house," I said. "After what happened to Sally Rachel and Mark, I thought if I could find out who it was we could stop these accidents. I didn't mean to go far, but the shadow just kept going. Pretty dumb, huh?"

"How did you get hurt?" Mark spoke up for the first time. His voice sounded scratchy, like it had rusted in his sleep.

"Something tripped me. Guess I wasn't paying attention to where I was walking. My arm doubled under me when I fell."

Mom sighed. "I think we all should go back to bed, and try to get some sleep," she said. "Joanna is not badly hurt. We can finish this tomorrow."

Her mouth was tight and her eyes suspicious, and I knew she wasn't satisfied with my story. However, she could tell I was in pain, so she didn't press me for more answers.

Mark dropped an awkward pat on my head as he went to his room.

"'Night, Joanna," Sally Rachel murmured, still crouched at my side. She dropped a light kiss on my knee, and gave me an "I love you" smile.

Sally Rachel said nothing after I had limped into the bedroom with Mom's help and turned out the light. I silently blessed her, because my arm hurt terribly and I ached all over. I knew she and Mark had dozens of questions. Tomorrow I'd have to have some answers.

I must have slept, because the sun was shining in the window when I opened my eyes. Everyone was gone but Mom, who had waited to take me to the doctor. My wrist was puffy, purple-colored, and very painful, but the x-ray proved her right. It was only sprained. The doctor gave me a sling to hold my arm more comfortably, and some pills for the pain.

Mom didn't ask any questions. She took me home and waited until Sally Rachel came at noon. Her silence was not a good sign. It was driving me crazy. Better to have her yell at me and get it over with.

When she left for the shop, she left strict orders we were not to leave the house. A few minutes later Mark came in.

"I got somebody to take my afternoon shift," he explained. "I had to know what happened last night. Come on, Joanna, spill it."

"Yeah, spill it," Sally Rachel echoed. "Who did you follow? Was it the witch?"

"I'm not sure." I hesitated. "What I think happened is too weird to have happened."

"Make sense, Joanna," Sally Rachel said sharply. "Start at the beginning. Why did you go into the woods? And why didn't you wake us up?"

Starting from the time I left the house to follow the shadow, I described, as best as I could, what happened. The part about the moaning and the dancing feet sounded even stranger than it seemed last night.

"I think I must have imagined that," I admitted. "I was probably still a little faint."

"Maybe," Mark said slowly. "Let's go over what we know. First, we find the stone house with the rotting teddy bears in the cellar. We see a scary face looking in the window."

"The witch," Sally Rachel said. "And she saw us."

Mark continued. "Next time we go, there's evidence someone else had been there trying to open the trap door. The teddy bears are okay, and we take the Indian necklace."

"Someone messes with your bike, and you have a wreck. Sally Rachel sees the witch and falls in the lake," I added. "I follow a shadow into the woods, trip over something — or was tripped — and sprain my arm. What are the odds of three people in the same family all having an accident in the space of ten days?"

"Oh, man, too big to call coincidence," Mark

said. "In both yours and Sally Rachel's "accidents" this spook was present. If the face in the window belongs to the spook, and if the same spook tried to open the trap door, then there must be something in the cellar it wants. The weird wails and dancing feet Joanna heard sounds like some kind of Indian ceremony. Maybe it's the necklace the spook is after."

"Why was the necklace on the teddy bear?" Sally Rachel asked, frowning. "Indians don't seem to go with teddy bears. Will she come after us if she finds it's gone?"

"I don't know," Mark said. "There's too much we don't know."

"How can we find out?" I asked warily. My arm was aching, and I wasn't sure I wanted to know. This talk about Indians and ceremonies made me nervous. I had visions of red-skinned devils casting spells.

"We can catch the spook and ask it," Mark proposed.

"I have a feeling that could be dangerous," Sally Rachel said with a shudder. "And it's not a spook, it's a witch Indian and she's already attacked us. She pushed me in the lake and tripped Joanna. She probably did the job on your bike too."

"I think Mark's right," I said, trying to slow down Sally Rachel's runaway conclusions.

"I don't know what I followed, but I never saw anybody walk like that. Maybe 'spook' is right. I'm not sure it wasn't just a shadow, a trick of light. How are we going to catch something like that?"

"I have an idea," Mark said, looking like someone had just turned on his light bulb. "Here's what we'll do . . ."

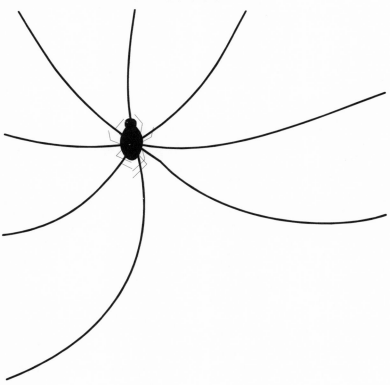

We Find An Ally

Mark's plan was simple.

"Whoever — or whatever — it is obviously wants to get into the cellar, but it can't open the trap door. We open the door, wait until it goes down, and then shut it in. We don't let it out until we find out what it is, and what it wants," he explained, looking pleased with himself.

"That means we'll have to be there when it finds the open door," I pointed out. "How do we know when it will decide to try again?"

"We don't. We go at a different time each day and wait. Sooner or later it'll come," Mark said.

"But that could take weeks!" I complained. "I have a feeling Mom isn't going to let us out of her sight long enough to spit, much less catch a spook," Sally Rachel said.

"Have you told your mom everything yet?" Mark asked.

"She won't listen and I wish I could get it over with. Thinking about it is almost worse than doing it," I admitted. "I think Mom and Aunt Laura *should* know what we're doing. Next time we might need some help."

"Maybe," Mark said reluctantly. "Sometimes parents only add to the problem."

"Your plan sounds great," I said, switching the subject off of parents. "I think we should try it."

"Me too," Sally Rachel added.

We all jumped when Mom suddenly appeared in the doorway. "I don't know what's going on," she said sternly, "but I don't want you "trying" *anything*. Whatever you kids have stumbled into is getting too dangerous for you to handle. It's a good thing I had to come back for my keys. Whatever this — this plan is, you can just forget it!"

"Mom, let me tell you —"

"I don't want to hear it now, Joanna. I haven't the time, and I can't cope with anything else. Your father will be here Friday night. Until then, you and Sally Rachel are restricted to the house and the shop. Understood?"

"Yes, ma'am," we answered in unison. Mom had reached her limits. Without another word, she picked up the keys off the mantle and left.

"Daddy will understand," Sally Rachel whispered after an awkward silence. "It's only one more day until he's here."

Dad was a special features reporter for the *Dallas Morning News*. He wrote articles about odd things that happened to people. He liked to brag that he had a "newshound's nose" for unusual news.

"I've sniffed out many a story others have missed," he'd say so charmingly that no one minded his bragging. Mom said he could charm a fence post if he put his mind to it. If anyone would understand, he would. One more day wouldn't make any difference.

I was excused from work the next day because of my injuries. I spent the day resting and trying to remember details so I could tell Dad exactly what happened. The more I thought about it, the less sense it made, and by afternoon my head was splitting.

Just before supper, Dad called and said a new story had broken and, of course, he had to stay with it. He couldn't make it until next weekend.

It threw us all in the dumps. A whole week to wait! Seven more days of being restricted to the house and shop. Seven more days of Mom's unhappy, suspicious looks. Worst of all, a whole week for our "spook-witch" to work without interruption at getting in the cellar. If the necklace was what the spook wanted, what would it do when it found the necklace was gone?

Each day was forever. Everybody was tense and jittery. Thank goodness the shop was busy enough to keep Sally Rachel and me from having too much time to think. My arm was very sore and useless and I still limped a little, but there were things I could do to help customers.

Mark could have gone to the stone house and kept on with the investigation, but he didn't. He spent a lot of time with Lester. They did jobs together. We watched them sometimes laughing and joking, sometimes talking seriously. Mark was more relaxed than he had been since we came. Maybe Lester *was* good for him. Seeing his warm smile and kindness to Mark almost made me forget my automatic dislike for him.

Several times I tried to tell Mom about the cellar, but something always stopped me. I finally gave up. I'd just have to wait for Dad.

The waiting was good in some ways. Mark's head healed. My wrist had gone from purple to greenish-yellow, though it was still a little swollen and painful to the touch. By Friday, we had been caged up so long we were about to explode. When Dad arrived just before suppertime, he noticed right away.

"Hey, what's wrong with my girls? This place feels like the inside of a pressure cooker. You better tell me all about it before you blow your corks," he said. His funny, lopsided grin switched on the dimple in his left cheek.

Like water bursting from a dam, the words poured out of everyone at once.

"Whoa!" Dad yelled over the din. "One at a time. Your mom told me what she knows over the phone. So Joanna, you start."

Taking a deep breath, I plunged in, starting with the day we found the stone house in the rainstorm. Before I finished, Sally Rachel and Mark were filling in details, and Mom andAunt Laura were looking more and more surprised. I ended with Mark's plan to trap the spook. This brought a loud protest from both Mom and Aunt Laura.

"Certainly not!" Mom declared firmly. "I should think you've had enough of this creature without trying to catch it. There's no telling what it would do if it's cornered."

"I agree," Aunt Laura added just as firmly. "Mark, I want you to stay away from it. We

74

have enough problems without you creating more."

Dad had been listening silently with his eyes half-closed and his hands behind his head in his "thinking position."

"Now, Ginny darlin', hold on a minute," he said to Mom.

Hope returned. When he called Mom "Ginny darlin'," it meant he was about to use his special gift of persuasion. Besides, I saw his newshound's nose begin to twitch.

"Dave, you can't mean you agree with this wild idea!" Mom said angrily. "These children have already been threatened and hurt by this — thing. Nothing is worth putting them in more danger."

"I don't mean to put them in any danger," Dad said. "Let's look at the facts. Whatever else it is, it looks old, right?"

"Right!" we responded.

"From what you've said, it is unable to open the trap door by itself. Seems to me Mark's plan is a good one. If they get it into the cellar, there's no way it can get out, unless they let it out. Let me know when you catch it. There might be a good story here."

"You're going to let them try to capture that . . . that whatever it is?" Mom's voice was almost a squeak. She gulped, shut her eyes, and said in a more normal tone, "I should have known you couldn't resist. Is there anything I can say that would change your mind?" She threw her hands in the air in frustration.

"Nothing at all, darlin'," Dad said. Grabbing one of her hands and sliding his other arm around her waist, he waltzed her around the room, loudly humming "The Blue Danube Waltz."

We giggled, and even Mom began to smile. He whirled her neatly to a stop by the kitchen door and asked, "Is there any food in this house? I'm starved!"

In the excitement, we had forgotten about dinner. We got busy warming up cold food and getting everything on the table. In spite of the confusion, Dad managed to take a good look at my arm, examine Mark's healing scar, and swing Sally Rachel up in a nuzzly hug. Oh, it was so good to have him home!

After dinner, we talked some more.

"Tomorrow, I want to see this stone house," Dad said. "I'd also like to see that necklace."

Sally Rachel ran to get it, and conversation stopped until she brought it back, sealed in its plastic bag. Dad carefully took it out and examined it.

"Mark's right," he said at last. "This is an

Indian fetish, probably Navajo. I've never seen one so beautifully made. I didn't know there were Indians in these parts."

"I found out a little bit about that in the library," Mark said. "There were Alabama-Coushatta Indians in this part of Texas years ago. I don't know if they had fetishes like this or not. It looks like Navajo to me too. They used them as charms to protect themselves from almost everything."

I was surprised. I didn't know Mark had taken time to go to the library. He had to go to Kennard to find one.

"Why did they leave it behind, if it was so important? Are Indians witches, and do they play with tea sets and teddy bears?" Sally Rachel asked, her eyes full of questions.

"Who knows? Maybe you'll find out," Dad said. "I think it's time for some sleep. I'm beat."

I went to bed relieved, and yet more confused than ever. What was this thing with a witch's face that floats instead of walks? What was its interest in the stone house? What did moldy teddy bears have to do with it?

As I drifted in that dreamy space between awake and asleep, I thought about Sebastian "Rusty" Carter. I hadn't seen him since the night of the dance. Was that enchanted bit of time before Sally Rachel's accident only a dream? As I tried to remember each delicious feeling of that night, the enchantment was swept away in another nightmare of cold, gray fog full of shadows and vines with snake faces that snapped at my ankles.

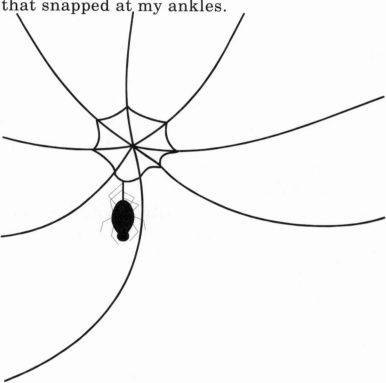

Setting the Trap

The next day was Saturday, and Mom insisted we help in the shop during the busy morning hours. Mark had to work, too, so we resigned ourselves to wait a little longer to put our plan into action.

The morning dragged, in spite of a pretty good crowd of shoppers. By lunch time we were wound as tightly as springs, and I thought Sally Rachel would take off like a rocket.

Aunt Laura volunteered to wait at the shop and take a late lunch. When Sally, Mom, and I got back to the house, Dad was working on a cup of coffee and chuckling over a TV cartoon. In bare feet and blue jeans, he didn't look much older than Mark. He pulled Mom onto his lap.

"Daddy, why aren't you ready?" Sally Rachel asked furiously. "We have to get the trap set!"

"Go get your lunch," he mumbled into Mom's neck. "There's plenty of time."

Mom looked kind of stiff, and I knew she was still against our plan. Maybe a little "kiss and hug" time with Dad would change her mind. I steered Sally Rachel toward the kitchen.

"Come on, let's fix lunch," I said. "We've got all afternoon to set our trap."

We were spreading mayonnaise for sandwiches when Mark stomped in, his face red, his jaw set. I thought at first he was just mad, but on closer look, I saw that he was fighting tears. He threw himself in a chair and buried his face in his hands.

"Mark, what's wrong?" I asked.

He didn't answer. For a long minute or two, he sat hunched and silent. Sally Rachel and I watched helplessly. When he brought his hands down, his face was under control, his mouth in a stiff, hard line.

"What's for lunch?" he asked gruffly, clearing his throat.

"Ham sandwiches. Be ready in a minute,"

I replied. I figured now was not the time to ask questions.

Dad strolled in and slapped his hand on Mark's shoulder. He had put on shirt and shoes, and combed his hair.

"Come show me your bike," he said. "Let's see if we can fix it."

Mark nodded awkwardly, like his neck had turned to wood. "Okay. It's out back."

"What brought that on?" Sally Rachel asked in dismay when they had gone.

"He must have walked in on Mom and Dad," I replied. "I guess it made him feel bad about his parents."

When Dad and Mark came back forty-five minutes later, Mark's eyes were red, but he was more relaxed.

"You okay?" I whispered.

"Better," he said with a twist of his mouth that was almost a grin.

While we ate, we talked about Mark's plan. We decided that late afternoon would be a good time for our first try. Mom was quiet, but she seemed more agreeable than before.

"Can't you hurry?" Sally Rachel said impatiently. She practically bounced off the walls with excitement. "Why do men have to be so slow?"

"Hang on, Sweet Pea, we're coming fast as

we can," Dad said. "A man can't think without food."

"I have a feeling it might rain. We have to hurry," Sally insisted.

"There go her feelings again," Mark groaned.

As if to prove her right, the sunlight faded and, for a moment, the room was tinged with gray.

The sun still played peekaboo around puffy, white clouds as we took the familiar path to the clearing. They were not yet rain clouds, but some of them were beginning to turn dark at the bottom.

Dad and Sally Rachel sang silly songs and told knock-knock jokes all the way to the clearing.

"Knock knock."

"Who's there?"

"Boo."

"Boo who?"

"Well, you don't have to cry about it!"

"Knock knock."

"Who's there?"

"Deluxe."

"Deluxe who?"

"Deluxe Ness Monster!"

By the time we got there I was giggling helplessly, and even Mark was grinning.

The shifting sunlight and shadows did strange things to the old stone house. I thought I saw someone slide from the house into the trees as we came up. But there was no sign that anyone was there. The clearing looked and felt empty. In spite of our giggles, I had an attack of shivers and goosebumps.

Dad gave a low, surprised whistle. "I didn't know they made houses all out of stone in these parts."

I guess I hadn't mentioned that the whole house was made of stone, and not just the floor. Come to think of it, we had not seen another like it since we'd been here.

"What's that?" Sally Rachel demanded, pointing to the doorway. She stopped dead, and Mark nearly ran her down.

Over the door hung a fetish necklace like the one in Sally Rachel's drawer. This one was much newer, and at its center was a bird with its wings spread. We looked without touching it, and left it where it was.

"Looks like they are a bit late with the charms," Mark said dryly.

The trap door had been attacked again. Small chunks were broken off its stone edge, and the floor was scuffed. We hurried down the steps as soon as Mark and Dad got the door open. The cellar was still as it had been. No one had been in it.

"Oh good, we're not too late," Sally Rachel said with a sigh.

Mark and I went back to the kitchen room to make plans while Dad and Sally Rachel poked around the cellar.

"How are we going to work this?" I asked.

"I don't know," Mark said. He looked around thoughtfully. "We have to find someplace to hide where we can't be seen, but where we can see the cellar door."

The room next to the kitchen was mostly collapsed. The ceiling slanted clear to the ground. The top ends of its beams still leaned against the roof like giant pick-up sticks. They formed a narrow triangle of space next to the kitchen wall.

I stooped to look into the triangle space. The floor was covered with trash and bits of rock. Mark pushed through the fallen beams, scattering rubble as he went. The sun peeped through a hole above us, striking sparkles on something in the trash. I picked it up.

It was an earring, a showy piece of costume jewelry made of different colored stones. I couldn't tell whether they were real stones or just glass. But they were much too flashy for my taste.

85

Suddenly a beam shifted as Mark brushed past it. A piece of the roof fell with a crash. Dust sifted down on us.

"Be careful, Mark!" I shouted. "You'll make it all fall in."

He waited until things were still again, then he cautiously moved on.

Dad's head appeared at the top of the cellar steps.

"What happened?" he asked.

"A piece of the roof fell in," I said. "It's all right now." I dropped the earring in my pocket.

"I think your mother's right," Dad said in his most serious tone of voice. "Now that I've seen this place, I think you should stay out of it. It's not safe."

"Daddy!" Sally Rachel wailed. "We can't stop now! We have to find out why the teddy bears are here, and who left the necklace."

"I know how much you looked forward to solving a mystery, but I'll have to go along with your mom on this one," he said. "The teddy bears are not worth you getting hurt. What's already happened should be a warning."

"Are you ordering us to leave it alone?" I asked faintly.

"I'm telling you my opinion," Dad said.

He rarely "ordered" us to do anything. He and Mom believed we should learn to look at the facts, and make our own decisions as much as possible. It was not always an easy thing to do.

"You are old enough to use good sense. You know how your mother and I feel. You can see the dangers. Now I'm going back to the house. Talk it over on your own."

We watched glumly as he walked quickly away. He was giving us the privilege of making up our own minds, but he made it very clear what he wanted us to do.

"I knew if we told the grown-ups they would spoil things!" Sally Rachel grumbled.

"Parents are the pits," Mark spat.

It amazed me how Mark seemed to resent and grieve for his parents at the same time.

"It's only because they love us," I said weakly. I felt like crying. "I guess this wasn't such a good idea. We better call it off."

"We weren't told we *had* to stop," Mark pointed out. "He just said we *should* stop. I say we go ahead with our plan. Sometimes parents do things we don't want them to. They don't listen to our wishes. Sally's right. We shouldn't have told them about it."

"I agree," Sally Rachel said with a firm nod of her head.

I didn't know what to say. Mark looked determined. Sally Rachel's chin was up and her jaw stuck out stubbornly. I didn't think I could change their minds. Half of me agreed with them. The other half shouted that Mom and Dad usually knew what was best for us, and we should use that good sense Dad talked about. They took my silence for agreement, and once the plans were made, I was too chicken to back out.

Mark searched again for a hiding place. After a few careful minutes of pushing and pulling beams and boards in the triangle space, he found what he was looking for.

"Sally, see if you can fit in there," he said. "I've tested it, and it won't fall on you."

Sally Rachel eased herself over a two by four and into the space behind it. Sitting slightly hunched over, she fit pretty well.

"It's okay," she said a little nervously. "Hey, there's a hole in the wall and I can see the kitchen!"

"Right," Mark said. "Can you see the trap door?"

"Yep. I'm looking right at it," she answered.

"Good. Are you comfortable enough to sit there for a while?" he asked again.

"I guess so," she said. "It is a little cramped. I hope it won't take too long."

"Here's what we'll do. I will hide in the woods. Joanna, you need to be where you can see both Sally Rachel and me. When the spook goes into the cellar, Sally can signal you. Then you can signal me. Then we close the trap door, before it knows we are there."

"Won't she see me?" Sally Rachel asked.

"Not when I get through," Mark said.

He took a broken piece of board, and wedged it across the opening to the space. Sally blended into the shadows, and was practically invisible.

"How will she signal me?" I asked.

"Here's my hat," Mark said, handing Sally Rachel his soft cap. "Can your stick your hand through this hole and wave it?"

Sally took the hat, and slipping her small hand through the angle of two beams, shook it briskly.

"That's great. Joanna, find a place where you can hide and also see the hat."

I'm a lot bigger than Sally Rachel, and a spot where I could see, but not be seen, wasn't so easy to find. We finally settled on a place outside the fallen wall. By lying flat on the ground, I could see through spaces in the broken rocks and boards to Sally Rachel's hiding place. A laurel bush at the corner of the house hid me from the path. Taking the pink-flowered scarf that held my hair, I waved it above me.

"Great, man, I can see it fine," Mark called from behind a big pine tree a little ways off.

We went back to Sally Rachel's cubbyhole for final instructions.

"You'll have to be very still, Sally," Mark cautioned. "And don't fall asleep. We'll give it an hour or so, and see what happens."

"Let's hurry! I have a feeling she could come any minute," Sally Rachel urged.

"Places everybody," Mark said. He disappeared behind his tree.

I lay on my stomach behind the laurel, my chin propped on my fist, my eyes on Sally Rachel's secret cubbyhole. The shadows from the gathering clouds hid her completely. I couldn't see her unless she moved.

I hoped it wouldn't take too long. I was very uneasy about going against Mom and Dad's wishes. We almost always went along with their advice. At the same time, I felt a strong tug of excitement that was hard to resist.

By pushing up the bottom limb of my bush, I could see the path into the clearing. Thunder rumbled in the distance, and I sent up a silent prayer that this would all be over before it rained.

The waiting seemed like forever. The little clouds that came and went across the sky were a welcome relief. It wasn't long before the clouds thickened and blotted out the sun completely.

I wondered how long Sally Rachel could sit still. She was not known for her patience.

A raindrop hit my nose. I looked at Mark's tree, but couldn't see him. The rain sprinkled down harder, and a squirrel chattered angrily in the trees. I don't know how long we had been watching, but it was getting late. Nothing was happening, and I'd had enough.

I stood up and called, "Mark, let's go! We'll have to try again."

He stepped from his hiding place. "I guess you're right," he agreed with a frown. "We'll come back tomorrow. It was probably as long as Sally could sit still anyway."

But Sally Rachel was asleep. The excitement had done her in. When I shook her awake, she climbed stiffly out of the cubbyhole, muttering that she hadn't seen a thing.

We closed the trap door, and started home in the rain. I felt miserable and discouraged. What were we going to tell Mom and Dad? We had never gone against their wishes before. Was it worth more accidents to go on with something that might be just a wild goose chase? But the mystery was getting more and more mysterious and interesting. How could we stop now?

As we left the clearing, I sensed movement in the woods. A branch swayed. A twig snapped. When I looked, there was nothing there. It could have been a squirrel or a rabbit, but I didn't think so. Somebody was watching us.

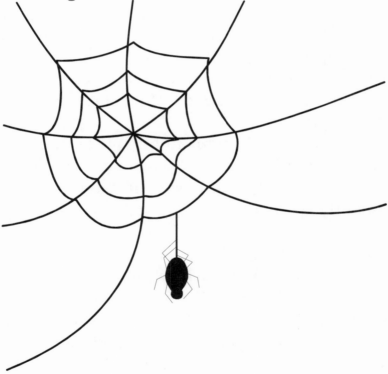

Sudden Scares

We hurried home silently, getting soaked in the soft, summer rain.

"It's only the first try," Mark said. "Don't anybody get discouraged. It might take several tries before we catch it."

He must have read my mind. I was certainly discouraged. I was about to say that I thought someone was watching us, and we should do what Dad said and stop the investigation. Suddenly I felt a thumping against my thigh.

It was the earring I found in the stone house. I had forgotten I put it in my shorts' pocket. I took it out and looked at it. The earning was very modern — big and heavy. I couldn't imagine anyone actually wearing it. It was nowhere in the same class as the lovely fetishes.

I wondered how it got in the stone house. Sometimes summer visitors explored the woods, not knowing that part of it is private property. Maybe one of *them* lost the earring. The thought of sightseers tramping in and out of the stone house was not comforting.

When we got home, Mom and Dad were waiting on the porch. Dad took one look at Sally Rachel and Mark's stubborn faces and my uneasy, half-apologetic one, and sighed.

"I see that you have decided to go ahead with this investigation," he said sharply. "Is that right, Joanna?"

I felt the blood rise to my hair roots, and knew my face and hair were the same color. A glance at Mark and Sally Rachel didn't help. They warned me with a glance. The earring dug into the palm of my hand.

"Y-yes, sir," I stammered against my better judgment.

"Very well," Dad said, his face very serious, his tone very solemn. "Your mom and I have talked this over. Since we have encouraged you to make your own decisions, we will honor this one — with a few restrictions. You have one week to wind this up. I'll be back next

94

weekend, and that will be the end of it. You will tell your mom or Laura where you are going at all times, and how long you expect to be gone. You will always stay together. No more going off alone. Understood?"

"Yes, sir," we mumbled.

"Good. The paper called, and I have to leave. I'll be back next Saturday, and I expect to hear you have been obedient. Now, come give me a hug so I can be off. You know I love you . . ." He paused, then said with a wink, "Good luck."

"Dave!" Mom protested with a little gasp.

"We have smart kids, Ginny," he said. "They will be okay."

"I have a feeling he doesn't think we will catch anything," Sally Rachel said when we had gone inside. "That's why he's letting us go ahead and try."

"Maybe," I said. "At least we have permission to keep trying. A week isn't very long. Think we can do it by next weekend?"

"Who knows?" Mark growled. "Grown-ups always have to put rules on everything. *They* come and go as they please. Why can't we do the same? Why can't they trust us?"

If Mom and Dad decided we could go ahead with this, they probably didn't believe any more harm could come of it. Excitement overcame my reluctance.

"They just don't want us to get hurt," I said. "Besides, look what I found. It was in the rubble near Sally Rachel's cubbyhole." I held out the earring.

"Oh man," Mark said, his eyes popping. "Where did that come from? Somehow I can't see our spook wearing it."

"Me neither," Sally Rachel added. "Not even a witch would wear that. Is it valuable?"

"Stones that big surely can't be real," I said. "It must be costume jewelry. But how did it get in the stone house?"

"Or maybe we have *two* spooks," Sally Rachel whispered. Her eyes were slits of suspicion.

"Or maybe a sightseer dropped it. It's heavy enough to pull an ear off," I said dryly. The earring was the clip-on kind. It could have easily fallen off. "Let's get back to Mark's plan. We only have a week."

"You're right, Joanna," Sally Rachel agreed. "When are we going back to the house?"

"I'm off from work tomorrow afternoon," Mark said. "Since we have to stay together, it's going to make it harder to find times to go. Think you two can take the afternoon off?"

"We'll try," I said. "We have to use every minute we can find."

Mom let us off at 3:00 with instructions to be home by dark. We set our trap again, feeling

96

that today would be the day our plan would work.

It wasn't. Nobody came near the clearing.

On Monday, Tuesday, and Wednesday we spent every minute we could, baiting our trap and catching nothing. Our frustration grew. Every day there was a new nick or two in the trap door. We held our breath until we made sure it had not been opened. Once or twice we saw a flick of moving shadow disappear in the trees as we came into the clearing. We were always too late to catch it.

The weather had turned hot and steamy. The laurel bush offered little protection from the sun. A colony of ants decided I was lying on their territory, and I fought a daily battle with them over the space. The ants always won, and I was slowly squeezed out of what spotty shade there was.

Squadrons of mosquitoes came out at sundown, making us miserable. There were no more accidents, but we were all jittery and nervous. We'd jump at the slightest sound, and everyone was cranky and out of sorts.

Several times on the way home, I sensed someone was following us. But I could never see who was there. There were rustlings and stirrings in the bushes that didn't seem natural. From the coner of my eye I saw movement that disappeared when I turned to look.

I guess it was mostly stubbornness that kept us from quitting. Since it was "our decision," we had to see it through. That, and the growing feeling that there was more to this than we first thought. The clearing quivered with tension. We knew somebody was coming to the stone house, but we could never catch her — or it — or whatever. *What would we do if we did?* I wondered with a shudder.

Thursday, Sally Rachel was clearing her cubbyhole of broken rocks, when she yelled, "Hey guys! Look what I found! Somebody left a bag here."

Mark and I hurried from our hiding places to look. She held a soft, brown leather bag that looked like a marble bag. When Mark opened it and turned it upside down, we couldn't believe what fell out.

Money. Coins and tightly wadded bills tumbled to the floor. And jewelry. The mate to the earring I had found was there, and lots of other earrings, pins, and rings.

"Oh man, this is the stuff that was stolen from the resort," Mark said with a gulp. "There's been talk about a thief, but nobody had any proof. There's little notices all over the bulletin board about missing money and jewelry. This is it!"

"Is our spook a thief?" I asked. "Is that

why it's trying to scare us off? Maybe it has nothing to do with the teddy bears and the necklace."

"Then who keeps trying to get into the cellar?" Sally Rachel asked. "And where did the other necklace over the door come from?"

"It might be trying to get in the cellar to find a better hiding place," Mark said. "The new necklace *is* a puzzle. It doesn't seem to fit."

"Neither do the weird, wailing sounds we heard," I pointed out. *Or the gliding thing I followed into the woods . . . or the dancing feet,* I thought. "We have to take this to the police. If we don't, we might be accessories to a crime."

"What's 'accessories?'" Sally Rachel asked.

"Helpers," Mark said. "We'll be as guilty as whoever stole it."

"Oh." Sally Rachel thought this over for a minute. "You know what will happen if we tell the police, don't you? They will come and take everything for evidence. We won't have another chance to find out who left the teddy bears and the necklace."

"She's right," Mark said quietly.

"If the thief is the spook we're after, then it's better for the police to handle it," I pointed out.

"Do you really think they are the same, Joanna?" Sally Rachel asked, a frown wrinkling her forehead.

"No. Not really," I admitted after a moment. "I can't believe that anyone who has something as beautiful as the fetish over the door would fool with this kind of stuff." I held up the earring that matched the one I found.

"I have an idea," Mark said. "We have only two more days to go. We could just leave the bag where Sally found it until Monday, and then turn it in. I don't see how two days would make any difference."

"Sounds good to me," Sally Rachel said. "How about you, Joanna?"

"I don't know," I wavered.

It didn't feel right. The law says to report stolen property immediately. But then, somebody had been collecting this for weeks. Would it *really* matter if it were reported Monday, instead of today?

Again they took my silence for agreement, and Sally put the bag back where she found it. I didn't object, and wondered if I would be sorry. Finding the bag complicated things. Our little mystery was turning out all wrong.

The next day it was drizzling rain again, but we decided to go ahead with our watch anyway. Since it was the last day, Mom was generous and gave us the whole afternoon off. Mark switched days with a friend and was also free. He was grumpy because Lester

100

Murray had left suddenly, without saying good-bye.

"Said he was going to see his father," Mark grumbled.

"You should be glad for him," I said, trying to soothe him. "You can write to him."

"He didn't leave an address," Mark said. "He just left."

"Well, maybe you will hear from him soon," I muttered.

It was too hot for raincoats. We put on old clothes, and let the warm rain soak us. Nothing was disturbed at the stone house. We took our positions and waited.

I had almost dozed off when Sally Rachel let out a shriek that jarred me to my feet. Mark and I both ran for the door. Sally Rachel was half in, half out of her cubbyhole, holding her knee and sobbing. Blood ran down her leg and into her sandal.

"Sally, what happened?" I gasped.

She was trembling all over. "I was trying to get more comfortable and cut my leg on a rock," she said through chattering teeth.

The cut didn't look deep, but it was bleeding badly. I tied my scarf tightly around her leg.

"Come on, Sally," I urged. "See if you can stand on it."

She could, but just barely. The cut was right where her knee bent and she couldn't walk on it.

"Let's make a seat with our arms," I said to Mark. "We can carry her."

"Joanna, Mark can get me home," she said through her tears. "You have to stay here and watch. It's our last chance! We can't miss it because of me!"

"We have to stay together. Remember? Besides, you'll need some help to clean that up when you get home."

"Sally's right," Mark said. "I can get her home and call Aunt Ginny. I'll be back as soon as she comes. It shouldn't take very long. Uncle Dave didn't count emergencies in the rules."

"But I can't lower the trap door by myself," I pointed out. "It wouldn't help for me to be here alone."

"You can see it," Sally Rachel insisted. "You can find out who it is."

I struggled with my feelings. The habit of looking after Sally Rachel was strong, but I could see that she was more scared than hurt. Blood always upset her.

"Please, Joanna," Sally begged. "Stay and watch. I'll be fine."

"Well, okay," I agreed reluctantly. Sally Rachel would be the one most disappointed if we gave up. What could twenty or thirty minutes hurt?

Mark swung Sally up on his shoulder, and she gave me a reassuring smile and a wave as they disappeared through the trees.

"Hurry back, Mark," I called, and was surprised at the squeak in my voice.

The rain had slowed to a fine mist. I tried to think what I should do. I wouldn't fit in Sally Rachel's cubbyhole. I decided the best place to wait was still behind the laurel bush. I could see the path from there, I'd be close to the door. The woods were very quiet. A shiver trembled through me.

Hurry, Mark, I thought. *Hurry! I don't like it here by myself.* I didn't worry about dozing off now. Every nerve in me was on alert.

Maybe ten minutes had passed, when I heard someone coming. *It can't be Mark,* I thought. *It's too soon.* And the sound came from the back of the stone house, not from the path.

I watched the door and waited. There was a thump, and two sneakered feet come out of the kitchen room. They must have come through the kitchen window.

I didn't know whether to let whoever it was know I was there or stay hidden. I decided it would look worse if they found me hiding, so I got up and tiptoed to the front door. I would pretend I had just walked up.

"Hello," I called brightly.

The intruder spun around. His shocked surprise was no greater than my own.

It was Lester Murray, and the stream of curses that spilled from his mouth made me wish I had stayed hidden. His face was sharp and ugly with anger. For a second, I thought he would strangle me.

Mark said he had left. What was he doing here?

After that first surprised moment, some of his charm returned. He smiled. "Joanna, what are you doing here? You scared me. Sorry about the language."

"I often come here," I said sharply. "It's part of Aunt Florrie's property. What do you want?"

It sounded rude, but I was too shaken to be polite. I never liked Lester, but I didn't suspect that he had such an ugly side. Even now, though his smile looked warm, his eyes didn't. A wave of fear washed over me. I had no idea what he would do.

"Mark told me about this place," he said smoothly. "Thought I would check it out. Fascinating old ruin. Don't you wonder who built it?" He put his hand up and shook the beam over Sally Rachel's cubbyhole.

"It's very interesting," I snapped. I wasn't

going to encourage conversation. I wanted him to go away.

"Where's Mark and your little sister?" he asked. His smile was now innocent and friendly.

"They're coming," I lied. "I walked on ahead."

He had moved closer, until he was standing right in front of me. The smile was still stuck in place, but a muscle in his jaw twitched like a jumping bean. His eyes glittered. He reminded me of a cat watching a careless squirrel.

I backed away nervously. Was he the kind who would attack a girl if he caught her alone?

"I'll tell Mark you were here. He thinks you left town," I said, holding my voice steady with an effort.

"I changed my mind," he said. "Come on. I'll walk you back."

"I'm not ready to go yet," I said. "I'll wait for Mark and Sally Rachel." I backed off some more.

His smile mocked me. "Sure. See you later then."

With a flick of his hand, he disappeared around the back of the house in the direction he had come.

The Spook Returns

My knees gave way, and I slid to the ground with a thump. I was shaking inside and out. Why did Lester Murray have such an awful effect on me? He didn't actually *do* anything to be afraid of. Lots of people use bad language when they are in a temper. I wondered if Mark had ever seen his anger.

Awkwardly, I got to my feet. I was heading for the laurel bush when Mark burst into the clearing.

"Everything's okay, Joanna," he called. "Aunt Ginny wasn't too happy that Sally Rachel was hurt, and she was upset we left you here by yourself. I had a hard time talking her into letting us stay until dark. What's the matter? You look funny."

"Your friend Lester was here," I said slowly, trying to control the squeak in my voice.

"He couldn't be. Lester left yesterday," Mark stated flatly.

"He said he changed his mind," I said. "He came through the kitchen window. Why did you tell him about this place? This was supposed to be *our* secret!"

Mark bristled, shocked at my outburst. "I didn't tell him anything important. Just that we had found an old house in the woods. What happened, Joanna? Why are you so upset?"

"Lester was really angry when he saw me here," I said, hugging myself to stop shaking. "He said awful things. He scared me."

"You were scared of Lester? Now I *know* you've got the wrong person. Lester wouldn't hurt a fly. Must have been a tourist you saw."

"It was Lester Murray I saw," I insisted. "He's not a nice person, Mark."

"Look, don't pick on my friends," Mark snapped. "If it *was* Les, you misunderstood him, that's all. Maybe we better just go home and forget investigating for today."

"Yeah, maybe we better," I agreed.

I tried to forget Lester Murray. After all, Mark knew him much better than I did. Maybe my feelings were wrong this time.

107

Saturday morning, Sally Rachel was too excited to sit still. A couple of stitches and a large bandage took care of the cut on her knee, and she was raring to go. Dad would be here tonight, and this was our last day to catch the spook.

After yesterday, I was not thrilled about going back to the clearing again. At the same time, I was determined not to let a creep like Lester Murray spoil our plans.

After a couple of clumsy, distracted hours at the shop, Mom let us go.

"You are not much help here anyway," she said. "Just be careful. I don't want any more casualties."

We opened the cellar door, and Mark disappeared behind his tree. Sally Rachel climbed into her cubbyhole, carefully avoiding the rocks. I took up my post under the laurel bush, well away from the victorious ants. Clouds were building in the west, but for now the sun was out, and the little clearing was cheerful.

I almost dozed in the warm sun. Minutes seemed like hours. Hours seemed like days. The clouds moved in — small, white, puffballs that bloomed into gray mountains hiding the sun. *Not rain again!* I thought. The thunderstorms didn't ever last long, but they came often, and were sometimes violent.

108

I looked up as fat drops splattered the ground. I pinched myself to be sure I was awake . . . because there it was! A cloaked and hooded figure stood at the edge of the trees, staring at the house.

The spook had come.

I was instantly alert and hoped Sally Rachel was not asleep again. The figure stood still as stone for a while, watching, almost sniffing the air. Then, moving in that strange off-the-ground walk, it glided across the clearing and in the door.

A moaning sigh that made my skin crawl came out of the kitchen. It must have discovered the open trap door. An instant later, I saw Sally Rachel's hat flutter in the gloom. Mark was already moving, and we slipped softly into the kitchen. The singsong chanting poured from the cellar. It sounded creepy and very sad.

Mark and I lowered the trap door, and Sally slid a board under it. She left just enough space to see into the cellar. The chanting stopped for an instant, then changed to a fearful wail. I shined the flashlight into the dark hole and stared in shock.

The terrified face I saw was not the one I expected. The horror in the black eyes couldn't hide the fine features and smooth white hair of the lady in the blue dress we had seen in the shop.

Sally Rachel's startled "Oh no!" and Mark's "Oh man! That's not the spook!" came at the same instant.

This was not the creature with the witch's face and frizzy hair. I couldn't imagine this dignified lady attacking anybody.

But it *had* to be the spook. The black cloak, the strange chanting, the peculiar walk — there couldn't be more than one, could there? Yet the face framed in the propped up trap door was definitely not the one we saw framed in the kitchen window. I stared in complete confusion. Had we made an awful mistake?

"Please, let me out," she begged in a quivery voice. "I didn't intend to hurt you. You frightened me."

I looked at Mark and Sally Rachel, and saw they were as stunned as I was. Her words suddenly struck me. *"I didn't intend to hurt you,"* she had said. Then she *was* the spook! Or at least the cause of the "accidents" we had.

"You admit you caused the accidents?" I asked.

"I had to get into my house. You frightened me," she repeated. "Please, don't shut me in down here."

She sounded really upset. Her voice shook as much as the hand that gripped the top step. Was she just pretending so we'd let her out?

Sally Rachel frowned. "You don't look like the thing who made me fall in the lake. But you are wearing its cloak. Did you find it somewhere?"

The woman's face turned even paler, and she took several deep breaths. She looked like she would faint.

"Please," she gasped. "Let me out."

I didn't see how this lady could possibly be the person we were trying to catch, no matter what she was wearing. She sounded so pitiful. I squashed my fears.

"Let's get the door, Mark," I said. We opened the trap door all the way back, and Mark cautiously held out his hand to help her up the steps. She came slowly, watching us suspiciously. She looked around as if expecting something or someone else. She clung to Mark's hand and breathed deeply again. A little color came back to her face.

Sally Rachel and I backed away, not knowing what to expect.

Mark cleared his throat. "I'm Mark Spencer, and this is Joanna and Sally Rachel Roberts, my cousins."

"We're trying to find out who left the teddy bears in the cellar," Sally Rachel explained in

111

a rush. "They must be important because a witch tried to scare us away." No polite chit-chat for Sally.

To my astonishment, the dark eyes lost some of their fear. She smiled.

"Oh, my goodness," she said with a faint chuckle. "Is that all you wanted? Perhaps we better talk. My name is Lily Morgan. Can we go somewhere and sit down? I feel a bit shaky."

"Are you an Indian?" Sally blurted out.

Lily Morgan smiled again. "Yes, indeed, I am. I belong to the Navajo tribe. My Indian name is Pale Feather. How did you know?"

"Mark says the necklace over the door is Indian, and the singing you do sounds like a war chant. You don't look like an Indian," Sally persisted. "The ones in the movies have dark skin."

"My father was a white man. I must have gotten my skin from him," Lily Morgan explained proudly.

"Let's take Ms. Morgan back to the house," Mark suggested before Sally Rachel could strike again. "She needs a place to sit down and a cup of tea."

"It isn't far, and the rain has stopped," I said, recovering my senses. She *was* wearing the hooded cloak, and she was making that peculiar noise, but I didn't think she would hurt us. Anyway, it would be safer at home.

The shower had passed, but the sky grumbled and flashed, promising still more rain. The air smelled of wet moss, ferns, and pine. Lily Morgan leaned on Mark's arm, stumbling a little on the soggy ground as we left the clearing. She didn't fit my picture of an Indian any more than she did Sally Rachel's. I guess when you knew to look, you could see that the slant of her eyes, and the shape of her face was different. I found it hard to connect Lily Morgan with the gliding, silent creature I had followed in the woods.

Sally Rachel prowled impatiently, sometimes ahead, and sometimes falling behind. Walking backwards in front of us, she asked bluntly, "Are you a witch too?"

"Sometimes," the woman answered quietly.

My head snapped around to see if she had that little smile that grown-ups get when they tease us, but her face was solemn, and her eyes were dead serious. Sally Rachel looked puzzled and jogged out of sight down the path, stiff-legged on her sore knee.

I was uneasy and angry. How could I ever convince Sally Rachel there is no such thing as witches when people go around admitting to being one? Was this person *really* a witch? If I had to describe a witch, it wouldn't look like her. But then, like Sally Rachel said, "Witches can look anyway they please." Can they? Do they exist in different forms? My thoughts scared me, and I moved a step or two away from Lily Morgan.

The surprises were not over. Mom was home, and when she saw our captive her face lit up with a surprised smile.

"Why, Ms. Morgan, where did they find you?" she exclaimed. "It's nice to see you again."

Sally Rachel, Mark, and I froze in our tracks. Mom gave us a strange look and took Lily Morgan into the house. *Mom knew her?* I couldn't believe it! Things were making no sense.

"I don't get it," Mark muttered under his breath.

"Me neither," I whispered. "It's weird."

"I have a feeling it's going to get weirder," Sally Rachel mumbled.

There wasn't time to figure it out. Mom had seated Ms. Morgan in a comfortable chair and was busy in the kitchen with tea things. Lily Morgan sat with her eyes closed, as if exhausted. She looked up with a thin smile when Mom brought the tea tray and poured a steaming cup for her. Sally Rachel, Mark, and I each got a glass of lemonade.

"Where did you find Ms. Morgan? I thought you were going to the stone house." Mom looked at us suspiciously.

"Mom, Ms. Morgan was at the stone

house. She's the spook and the witch," Sally Rachel said.

Mom looked astounded. "You're joking, I hope!" she said angrily. "Lily Morgan is a well known silversmith. She brought some of her jewelry to the shop one day. She is certainly not a spook — or a witch! How can you say such a thing?"

We all spoke at once, each trying to prove our point. In the racket no one paid any attention to Lily Morgan until her voice cut through the noise in a calm but firm statement.

"The children are right, Mrs. Roberts. Sometimes I am a witch."

The stream of words stopped as though someone had turned off a switch. All eyes were on our visitor.

There she sat, stringy hair straggling from beneath the black hood, her toothless mouth a sunken hollow between the hooked nose and pointed chin. Her hands were hidden in the cloak, pulling it close around her.

Thunder exploded overhead, and a blazing flash of lightning turned everything black and white. The thing in the chair put her head back and let out a shrieking laugh that turned my blood to ice.

The Changing Face

I heard a high-pitched scream and clapped my hands over my ears. Then Mark was holding me while Mom hovered anxiously. Everything was like a nightmare with people looking like underwater ghosts and sounding like a slowed-down record. They said it was me that screamed. I must have fainted.

As my head cleared, I looked fearfully at the chair where the witch was, but it was Ms. Morgan who sat there. Her hair was neatly in place, and her mouth full of teeth, her cheeks and chin rounded out. Her nose was still long and pointed, but it looked proudly noble, not witchy at all.

I decided I must be going crazy. I closed my eyes and shuddered.

"It's okay, Joanna, you're not crazy." Sally Rachel said, holding my hand and reading my mind. "Ms. Morgan was showing us how she could make herself look like a witch when she wanted to. All she did was take out her teeth and let down her hair. See, you were right. She's not *really* a witch."

For Sally Rachel to admit I was right was enough to drive the fog from my head. I sat up and looked closer.

"How do you know?" I asked suspiciously.

"Yeah, how do you know?" Mark repeated. "I didn't see that happen."

"While all of you were fussing over Joanna, I was watching Ms. Morgan. I was as scared as you, at first, but when you screamed, she put her teeth in, smoothed her hair back, and she's Ms. Morgan again."

I studied her through narrowed eyes, finding what Sally said hard to believe. How could such small things change a person's appearance so much?

"I think it's time for explanations," Mom said sharply. "If you are responsible for all the accidents that have happened, you better have a good reason. You could have killed my children!"

Mom's friendliness had vanished. She stood up and moved around the room in ner-

117

vous little jerks, turning on lamps in the darkening room. Hard rain sounded like rocks on the roof, and wind whooshed through the pines in a mournful moan. We drew closer together in front of Lily Morgan's chair, all eyes on her face.

"Why do you make yourself look like a witch?" Sally Rachel asked.

"The Navajo, or The People as they call themselves, believe everyone is a mixture of good and bad. Sometimes when we want something very much, the bad part tries to help," she explained. "I wanted you to think I was a witch to frighten you away."

"But why did you hurt the children?" Mom asked. "They did you no harm."

"I didn't mean to hurt the little one," Ms. Morgan said softly. "I would have pulled her out of the pond myself if you hadn't come in time. I didn't know she couldn't swim. You were all in and out of my house, and I couldn't get in the cellar. The other one is dangerous. I couldn't trust any of you. I just wanted to frighten you away."

There was so much pain in her voice, I found myself beginning to feel sorry for her. Then I realized what she said. Other one?

"What other one?" I asked, puzzled.

"The tall young man with hard blue eyes,"

118

Mrs. Morgan said. "He is wicked. I'm glad he is not here."

Tall young man with hard blue eyes. *Who is she talking about?* I wondered. There were several guys working at the resort who had blue eyes, including Rusty Carter and Mark. Obviously, it wasn't Mark she was talking about. I hadn't seen Rusty since the night of the dance. Sometimes I think I dreamed him up.

I glanced at Mark. He had a puzzled frown on his face.

Sally Rachel didn't seem to notice. "Were the teddy bears yours?" she asked bluntly.

"One of them was," Mrs. Morgan said. "The others belonged to . . ." she hesitated, ". . . other children I knew."

"Why did you leave them in the cellar?" Sally Rachel barged on.

"We were playing there one day when a terrible thing happened. Their mothers blamed my mother and me, and took their children away before they could go back and get the teddy bears." Her face drooped with sadness, and her voice was full of tears.

"What happened?" I heard myself asking tensely.

"There was a sawmill here then," she said with a sigh. "My father was a foreman there. Mother was a full-blooded Navajo, and Indians

119

were not liked or trusted. She and I were not accepted by the mill people. Her name was Red Feather, but Father called her Rose. He built the stone house for us out here away from the others. It was the only house that had a cellar." She smiled wistfully, remembering.

"Father was killed in a mill accident," she went on. "The day the children were there, the women had come to bring food and condolences. The custom was strong among the mill towns, even for those they didn't accept. All the children brought their favorite toy, the teddy bears. They were Christmas gifts from the mill managers that year.

"While they were with us, there was an explosion at the mill, and more men were killed. The women blamed Mother and me because we were 'the Heathens in their midst.' They snatched their children up, and in seconds they were gone. I was only four years old, but I will never forget the ugly words and the hatred on their faces.

"Everyone forgot about the teddy bears. Mother and I left that same day. I haven't been back until now."

"Were you looking for your necklace?" Sally Rachel asked.

Lily Morgan jerked around. "Do you have it?" she asked sharply.

"It's in my drawer. I'll get it," Sally Rachel said, scrambling to her feet.

She was back in a minute, and she laid the plastic bag in Ms. Morgan's lap.

"We didn't steal it," Sally explained. "We just wanted to keep it safe until we found out who left it in the cellar."

Ms. Morgan opened the bag and gently took out the necklace. She stroked each carved animal lovingly between her fingers. Holding the necklace to her face, she closed her eyes and crooned in that singsong manner we had heard before. No one spoke or moved. The force of her feelings held us speechless.

Then she spoke, her words breaking the spell.

"You don't know how much it means to have this back. When it wasn't in the cellar, I thought it was lost forever. I can't thank you enough for keeping it."

"It means a lot to you, doesn't it?" Mark said softly.

"Oh, yes. Grandmother gave this necklace to Mother when she married. She knew she would have a hard time in the White Man's world. It was her protection. Mother put it around my neck when Father died. It is very old and very precious."

"Why did you put it on your teddy bear?" Sally Rachel asked.

"To protect him. I loved that teddy bear, and so many bad things were happening. The fetish was meant to guard the wearer from harm. I put the new one over the door to protect the house, but it's not the same as this one."

"Ms. Morgan, I think we've missed something," Mark said thoughtfully. "You said you were the one that scared Sally Rachel into falling into the pond. Did you fix my bicycle so it would wreck too?"

"Oh, my, no!" Lily Morgan looked shocked. "I wouldn't know how to *fix* a bicycle."

"Why were you watching our house the night I followed you into the woods?" I said.

"I was resting, not watching," she said. "The walk around the pond was farther than I thought. I tire quickly. I was so afraid you would catch me. When you tripped and fell, I did a healing dance for you until you woke up. Then I followed you home to be sure you got there safely."

"If you didn't break my bike, then who did?" Mark asked. "Who else is warning us off and why?"

"Could your bike wheel have come loose by itself?" Mom asked.

"No way," Mark declared. "I had checked it

that morning. Besides, there was the note telling us to mind our own business."

"I still have a feeling we have more than one spook," Sally Rachel said darkly.

A crash of thunder underlined her words, and the lights went out.

Truth in the Darkness

Before we could recover, the front door burst open, and Aunt Laura swept in with the wind and rain.

"Sorry I'm so late," she called out, struggling to close the door. "I tried to wait until the rain let up, but it kept getting worse. Can't we get some light? I can't see a thing. Ginny? Mark? Is anybody there?"

Dazzled by the sudden darkness, we were slow to react. At the sound of her name, Mom stirred.

"I'll find some candles," she said, stumbling over my feet as she groped her way to the kitchen.

"I'll get the matches," Sally Rachel volunteered.

When the candles were lit, Aunt Laura gave a startled gasp.

"Why, Ms. Morgan, how nice to see you. Did you come about the jewelry?"

"Seems like I have stepped into the middle of a small mystery," Ms. Morgan said with a shaky laugh.

"Mystery? What mystery?" Aunt Laura asked. "Oh, don't tell me the children have gotten you involved in the teddy bear thing."

"Yes, one of the bears is mine. But it seems now there is someone else involved."

"Ms. Morgan was the person who scared us, and made Sally Rachel fall in the pond. But she had nothing to do with Mark's accident, or mine," I explained.

"It is the other young man with the blue eyes," Lily Morgan said. "He was at my house several times when I went there. He hid something in the bedroom. One day he threw stones at me when he saw me in the woods. He was very angry when he found me watching."

The leather bag! Lily Morgan had seen the thief hiding the leather bag.

"Do you know who this person is?" I asked.

"He works at the pavilion. He's older than most of the boys, and has a charming way of hiding his true self. I have seen him with you quite a lot," she said, nodding at Mark. "I thought you were all together in this."

"Lester Murray," I murmured. The description fit. He must have come to collect his bag the day I saw him at the stone house.

I looked at Mark. He hadn't said a word since the lights went out. I could tell by the struggling expressions on his face that he didn't want to believe what she said.

"It can't be. Les was out of town the day you said you saw him, Joanna. He told me so," he muttered. "Besides, he wouldn't hurt me. He's my friend."

"We found a leather bag in the stone house full of money and jewelry," I explained. "Apparently it was stolen from people at the resort. We decided to leave it there until tomorrow. It was our last chance to find out about the teddy bears," I finished lamely.

"Joanna! You should have called the police at once!" Mom exclaimed. "This is much more serious that your little mystery!"

"I know," I admitted, squirming a little. "We thought one more day wouldn't hurt."

"That's what Les was doing at the stone house when you were there, Joanna," Sally Rachel said. "He came to get the bag."

"You're wrong!" Mark shouted. "Les is not like that. He would never steal. He's my *friend!*"

"He pretended to be your friend when you needed a friend. He was probably the one who messed with your bike. If he was using the stone house to hide his 'loot,' he certainly didn't want us snooping around," I said gently.

Mark sat shaking his head, his face twisted in stubborn disbelief.

"There's nothing we can do about Lester tonight," Mom said softly, patting Mark's shoulder. "The telephone is out too. I tried to call Dave a little while ago."

"Where did you and your mother go when you left here?" Sally Rachel asked, bringing us back to Lily Morgan's story.

"We went to Mother's people in New Mexico. In the custom of the Navajo's, her sister's husband married her as a second wife."

"I bet you were glad to be with Indian children and have friends again," Sally Rachel remarked.

"The Navajo children were as cruel as the white children," Ms. Morgan said with a sigh. "They named me Pale Feather because I was only half Indian. I learned to do without friends. Even though it was not the custom then for Navajo women to work with silver, my uncle taught me the craft. I spent all my time with him."

I felt a rush of sympathy. Ms. Morgan didn't fit in as Pale Feather any better than she had as Lily. She was rejected by everyone.

Shame flooded out the sympathy when I remembered how out of place I felt in my family. My problem was *nothing* compared to hers.

"Why did you come back?" Sally Rachel asked.

"My Grandson was coming to East Texas to check on our customers. He is in charge of the jewelry business now. I knew it would be the last chance to find the fetish. There was no suitable time to come sooner." Her voice faded out, and I could see she was very tired.

The storm was gone, trailing faint rumbles of thunder and brief, pale lightning behind it.

"I'll drive you back to your cabin, Ms. Morgan," Mom said quietly.

Before Lily Morgan could get out of her chair, the door burst open again, and Dad came in.

"There's police cars at the Pavilion," he said loudly. "Looks like they've caught a thief . . ."

He stopped short when he saw the candlelit room and the spellbound group staring at him.

"What's happened?"

"The lights went out," Sally Rachel piped

up. "This is Lily Morgan . . . Pale Feather. She was our spook, only she didn't hurt Mark's bike or make Joanna fall in the woods. And she's not really a spook. There's another spook that broke Mark's bike and hid the jewels in the stone house . . ."

"Whoa! I better go out and come in again," Dad said with a laugh. "Somebody else please explain."

Mom took charge, introducing Dad to Ms. Morgan, and giving a thumbnail sketch of what had happened. When she finished, Mark asked hesitantly, "Do you know who the police caught?" Mark's face was strained, and he looked like he was holding his breath.

"Some kid who worked at the pavilion. You might know him. His name is Lester Murray."

Mark groaned and buried his face in his hands.

"Uh-oh, you do know him, don't you?" Dad said, gently squatting down beside Mark, who still sat on the floor.

"I'm sorry, Mark. Was he a special friend? I'm afraid there's not much doubt that he did it. He was stopped for running a red light, and the police caught him with a bag of money and jewelry. All they need is some proof that he actually took the stuff, and didn't just find the bag somewhere."

"I'm afraid I can give them that," Ms. Morgan spoke up. "I saw him hide the bag."

"Oh, man, how could I have been so stupid?" Mark exclaimed grimly. He got up stiffly and went to his room.

Poor Mark! To find out you trusted someone who is dishonest is a terrible thing.

Mom and Dad drove Ms. Morgan back to her cabin. The electricity was still out, and we went to bed by shadowy candlelight.

Lily Morgan's story kept running through my mind, and it took me a long time to get to sleep. She was different from her people but she made a success of her life. And even though she pretended to be a witch to protect her property, she was not evil. The real evil was in the one who pretended to be a friend.

When I finally dreamed, I was the first redhead ever to become a Navajo. They called me "White Fire."

Burying the Past

"What I'd like to know is how Ms. Morgan moved the way she did? It was like she had wheels instead of feet." We were at lunch the next day, and I couldn't forget that peculiar gliding walk Lily Morgan used.

"It's the way she puts her feet down and moves in a circular motion," Dad said. "It's an old Indian skill. Ms. Morgan's ancestors used it to track game when they had to hunt for their food."

"I wish she would teach it to me," Sally Rachel said.

She stepped across the room heel to toe, twisting her hips as she went. It was more a waddle than a glide, and she looked like a drunken duck.

131

"Will we see her again?" I asked.

"I don't think so. Her grandson is taking her home this afternoon," Dad said.

"What are we going to do about the teddy bears?" Sally Rachel asked. "We can't just leave them in that old cellar."

"Why not?" Mark growled. "They've been there for years."

Mark had stayed in his room all morning, refusing to go to church with us. He appeared at lunch time looking sad.

Sally Rachel rolled her eyes at him, and said patiently, "They were waiting to be found so their story could be told. Now that it is, they want to be laid to rest."

"We'll have a funeral," I said, suddenly inspired. "We can bury them in the clearing next to the stone house."

"Hhmp!" Mark snorted. "A funeral for rotting straw? You've got to be kidding."

"It would be a way of showing respect to Ms. Morgan and the other children who left them there," Mom said softly. "There was a lot of pain in that house. Maybe that would release it."

I thought of the sadness I felt the first time we saw the stone house. Did Mom feel those things too? Maybe we were more alike than I thought.

"Sounds like a good idea, but I've got to go," Dad said. "I'd like to get back in time to write up the notes I made on Ms. Morgan's story. There's the robbery story too. It's been a fascinating weekend. I'll have to visit my family more often when they are on vacation."

There were hugs for all of us, including Mark, who was about as huggable as a post.

"Hang in there, Mark, Things will get better," Dad said.

"Sure," Mark mumbled.

The telephone chirped in the kitchen, and Aunt Laura went to answer it. She came back looking stunned, puzzled, and pleased all at once.

"That was your father, Mark. He wants to come and talk to us," she said.

"Oh, man," Mark groaned. "When is he coming?"

"Tomorrow. Don't get your hopes up," Aunt Laura cautioned. "He just wants to talk. I think he's lonesome."

Mark banged out the door without a word. I hurried after him.

"Mark, wait a minute," I called.

He acted like he didn't hear me, and I had to run to catch up.

"You said you wished your dad would come," I said, panting for breath. "What's wrong?"

"Yeah, I did," Mark mumbled through clenched teeth. "Now he'll find out how stupid I was about Lester. I must be an idiot! That guy set me up! *I* could have been arrested. He asked me to keep a package for him one day when he had to go to town. 'Don't let it out of your sight it's very important to me,' he said. And all the time I thought he was my friend! How could I have been so wrong? Dad'll never forgive me."

"Everybody makes mistakes," I said. "Even parents. You've pointed out how stupid *they* can be. Maybe you can forgive each other."

"Yeah, maybe," he agreed grudgingly. He made a hooting sound, something between a laugh and a howl.

Sally Rachel came running through the trees, skidding to a stop by my side.

"What's wrong with him now?" she asked.

"Just letting off steam," I said. "I think he'll be okay."

"I sure hope so," Sally said snippily. "How about the teddy bear funeral? Why don't we have it now?"

"Why not?" Mark said. "We can bury our mistakes with them."

"Good idea," I said. "I've got a few I'd like to see the last of too."

As we gathered the teddy bears into plastic bags, I wondered what we would do for excitement the rest of the summer. Our mystery was solved. The summer looked boring again.

But that night after supper, Rusty Carter called to ask me out for a Coke . . .

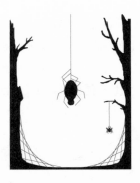

More about
the East Texas Piney Woods

The piney woods of East Texas are full of ghost towns, all created by the same thing — the lumber industry. In the late 1800s and early 1900s, lumber was in great demand to rebuild towns destroyed in the Civil War and to build new towns as people moved west and settled new territories. Greedy lumber companies bought up the forest lands and cut down all the trees without replanting or waiting on new growth. It was called clear cutting, because the land was literally cleared of everything on it.

The sawmills were located deep in the forests to be near their supply of trees. The company that owned the mill made a town for their employees. They built houses, supplied a doctor to tend to them, a minister to marry and bury them, and stores to shop in with the money it paid them. When people died, they were given a company funeral and were buried in a company plot.

The new railroads ran tram lines into the forest to carry the cut trees to the sawmill. The tram lines and the new steam skidders (a steam-powered winch with a steel cable to drag trees across the ground) made logging so easy that the companies got careless and cut too many trees too fast. When they ran out of trees, the mill closed and the town was abandoned.

Running out of trees was not the only reason a mill closed. Spark from the steam engines often set the sawdust on fire and burned the mill down. Sometimes the giant saws would overheat and literally explode. Competition for the precious trees was fierce, and now and then sabotage from a rival mill would get out of hand. If the destruction was more than the company could afford to replace, they simply left the mill and moved on. The town rotted away. Only a small graveyard or crumbling remains of the mill walls were left to show where it had once been.

Sometimes a mill closing did not mean sudden death for the town. An example is the village of Ratcliff in Houston County. In 1885 a settler from Georgia, Jesse H. Ratcliff, built a small sawmill in his community. The little town grew and was given his name.

In 1899 a man named R. H. Keith arrived and began buying up the land. By 1901 he had bought enough land in Houston and Trinity counties to support a major sawmill. He sold it to the Louisiana and Texas Lumber Company, and they kept buying land until they had 120,000 acres, including Jesse Ratcliff's little sawmill.

This huge mill was known locally as the Central Coal and Coke Company (called the Four C, or CCCC). As usual the company built houses for their workers and their own commissary store, where they expected their people to shop with special credit cards instead of money. The workers, however, liked the shops in Ratcliff. The management of the Four C didn't appreciate this competition, so they built an eighteen-foot fence between the mill and Ratcliff to keep their people home.

The merchants of Ratcliff, angry at this threat to their business, took to tying up the guards and dynamiting the fence, until the Four C Company gave up trying to keep a company-controlled town. After that, the mill and the town flourished, and by 1910, Ratcliff had 10,000 people. They say it was so crowded on Saturdays "you couldn't squeeze your way down the sidewalk."

But the Four C Company did not manage its lands wisely, and they soon used up all their trees. They were not able to buy more land close enough, so in 1920 the mill closed, leaving Ratcliff without its main source of jobs.

A few years later, the timberlands were sold to the federal government and were made part of the Davy Crockett National Forest. New trees were planted and the old Four C log pond was turned into a public camping area called Ratcliff lake. The town of Ratcliff hung on but dwindled to less than a hundred people living there now. The setting of *The Cellar in the Woods* is modeled after Ratcliff Lake.

While a remnant of Ratcliff still exists, many other mill towns are only a memory. Some of them had very interesting names:

Barnum in Polk County was named for the circus owner P. T. Barnum.

Cheeseland was known for its fine cheeses made by local families.

Fair Play got its name from the way travelers were treated at a local hotel and store.

Rake Pocket was named for the way it cheated people.

Pinetucky in Jasper County was named for the Kenuckians who settled the piney woods.

Pluck was so called because residents claimed it took a plucky man to stay there.

Seedtick in Nacogdoches County had lots of insects.

In 1995 the mills in East Texas were again expanding. Some of the forests in the Northwest were closed to harvesting because of the endangered habitat of the spotted owl, and the nation looked to Texas trees to meet the increased demand. Perhaps the one or two large companies who control the industry have learned a thing or two about conservation and land management, and will not create more ghost towns in the forests.

Glossary

Alabama Coushatta: a small tribe of Indians who lived in East Texas.

amethyst: a lavender or purple stone used in jewelry.

awkward: clumsy, ungraceful, embarrassing.

The Blue Danube: a waltz about a river in Europe.

boutique: small specialty shop that sells clothes

carnival glass: glassware first made around 1900. The glass has a rainbow effect in sunlight and was a popular giveaway at carnivals. Many pieces are still made today.

cellar: a room underneath a house, usually for the purpose of storing something; there are root cellars for canned food and wine cellars for wine; tornado cellars are a safe place to go in a storm.

chanting: singing one or two notes again and again.

chiseled: clean, sharp edges.

commissary: the company store.

concussion: an injury of the brain from a blow on the head.

coral: a red-orange stony substance secreted by corals used to make jewelry.

cults: a group of persons sharing a special interest.

cut glass: glassware decorated by cutting tools Decayed, rotted.

Depression glass: glassware made during the Depression years. It came in different colors and was sold very cheaply or given away as prizes or premiums.

dismally: gloomy, dreary.

dumps: feeling low, unhappy, depressed.

endangered habitat: the home of a living creature that is in danger of being destroyed.

fetish: a material object believed to have magical powers.

flustered: to be nervous or upset.

grizzled: gray-haired.

healing dance: a ceremonial dance to heal sickness or injury. The Navahos had dances for many things; blessings, war, good crops are a few.

impulse: a sudden urge or desire.

jet: a dense black coal that takes a high polish and is used in making jewelry.

laurel: a bush or shrub.

log or mill pond: source of necessary water for the mill.

monotonous: having one tone; the same thing over and over.

Napolean fashion: holding one hand inside a shirt between the buttons making a temporary sling; it was a favorite pose of Napolean Bonaparte.

Navajo: a major Indian nation.

newshound nose: able to 'smell out' or recognize a good story.

occult: dealing with the supernatural.

pavilion: canopy or shelter; building for social or recreational use.

penlight: a tiny flashlight the size of a fountain pen.

pick-up sticks: a game with long thin sticks that are dumped in a heap. Players use a black stick to carefully pick sticks off the heap without collapsing it.

piney woods: area of East Texas with thick forests of pine trees.

plague: a highly infectious and fatal disease.

pokey: slow, uninteresting.

pressure cooker: a special pot that cooks food very fast under high pressure.

recuperate: get well.

retail sales: selling things to the public as opposed to selling them to another store or business.

sabotage: an underhanded effort to harm or stop something from happening.

sarcastic: to mock or jeer at.

silversmith: someone who makes jewelry and objects out of silver.

tinged: having a slight color.

throwback: to revert to a former type of family characteristic.

tram lines: railroad tracks.

turquoise: a blue to blue-green mineral stone used in jewelry. Indians call it the Sky stone.

wangle: to use tricky or false methods.

wheedle: to persuade by being clever or tricky.

winch: a stationary motor-driven or hand-powered hoisting machine having a drum around which a rope or chain winds as the load is lifted.

woozy: dizzy, feeling sick.

* * * * *

Special thanks to Ali Clark, sixth grader at Woodrow Wilson School in Denton, Texas, for her help in compiling the glossary.

Bibliography

The Enduring Navaho
   Laura Gilpin
Skystone and Silver
   Rosek and Stacy
The Navaho
   Kluckholhn and Leighton
Crosscut
   Third Quarter, 1988
The 35 Best Ghost Towns in East Texas
   Bob Bowmen
Big Thicket Bulletin
   April, 1978